THE TIME TUNNEL

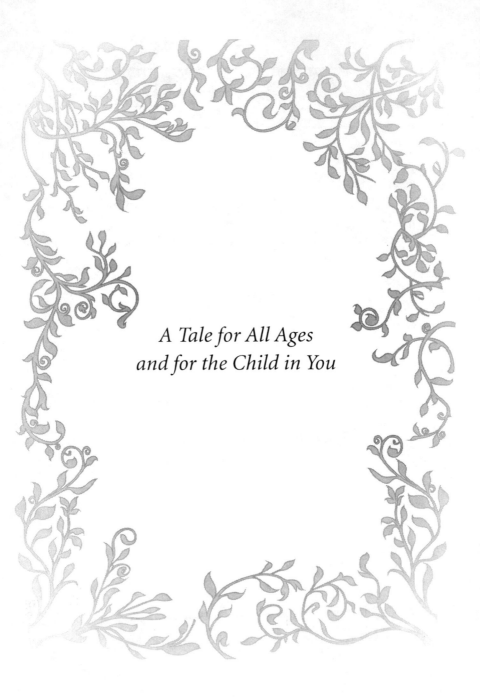

*A Tale for All Ages
and for the Child in You*

THE TIME TUNNEL

"Receive the kingdom of God as a little child...."
Mark 10:15

"For of such is the kingdom of God."
Luke 18:16

Swami Kriyananda

Crystal Clarity Publishers
Nevada City, California

Crystal Clarity Publishers, Nevada City, CA 95959-8599

Copyright © 2012 by Hansa Trust
All rights reserved. Published 2012

Printed in China
ISBN 13: 978-1-56589-101-2
ePub: 978-1-56589-502-7

1 3 5 7 9 10 8 6 4 2

Cover and interior design by: Amala Cathleen Elliott

Library of Congress Cataloging-in-Publication Data

Kriyananda, Swami
    The time tunnel : a tale for all ages / Swami Kriyananda.
        p. cm.
    ISBN 978-1-56589-101-2
        I. Title.

PZ7.K915Ti 2011
    [Fic]--dc22

                        2010019131

www.crystalclarity.com
clarity@crystalclarity.com
800-424-1055

*I lovingly dedicate this book
to the memory of my brother Bobby,
John Robert Walters.*

Table of Contents

Preface

By Asha Praver, author, teacher, lecturer

Two boys vacationing in the forests of the Transylvanian alps (the Carpathians) discover a ruined laboratory, a *recently* deceased dinosaur, and a mysterious humming tunnel. Whether fact or fiction (the author remains vague on the point), this book contains more truth than many a ponderous volume of philosophy gathering dust on a library shelf.

Yes, certain ideas presented here are intuited rather than proved. Who can say for *sure* how and why the Great Pyramid was built? Or what Atlantis was like before the island sank into the sea? Or whether man and insects in future ages will coexist respectfully, and window screens will no longer be needed?

Swami Kriyananda has earned the right to speculate on these and other fascinating aspects of past and future. As one of the most eminent spiritual teachers of our times, his intuition has been honed over more than six decades of devoted meditative practice.

In this story, young brothers, Donny and Bobby, guided by a grown-up named Hansel, travel back in time to meet sages, villains, and common citizens, then forward to an age of spiritual enlightenment only a sage like Kriyananda could imagine and describe.

The idea that time is an illusion, sustained only by our self-definitions, is a fascinating but bewildering concept—one about which I had long known, but barely comprehended, until Hansel patiently explained it in his answers to Donny's questions.

Maybe we can't build a time tunnel from the instructions in this book, but when such a thing is created, I believe it will resemble (at least in concept) what is described here. And what we find when we enter that tunnel and come out the other side—whether through the ruined laboratory in Transylvania or in the wilderness of our own consciousness—will be territory long familiar to the readers of this book.

Swami Kriyananda says he wrote this story mostly for the fun of it. So scroll up your time-light sphere (Oh, you don't know what that is? Read on: you soon will know!). Join Donny, Bobby, and the grown-ups Hansel and Swami Kriyananda himself on this delightful, *timeless* adventure.

Foreword

What is a writer of philosophical works doing, producing a work for children? Well, I have an honorable precedent in Lewis Carroll (Charles Dodgson)'s work, *Alice in Wonderland*. In my case, in an idle moment two years ago, I picked up a copy of *The Wizard of Oz* and glanced at the first pages. I came to the yellow brick road, which is almost at the beginning, when the thought came to me, "Why not write a book for children?" Really I must say, it wasn't *my* idea; the thought was, so to speak, *given* to me.

I sat down at my computer and asked, "All right: What is this story to be about?" And then the theme appeared. From then on I just sat back and let the ideas flow! In two weeks the story was written more or less as you see it here (though, like Donny and Bobby in the story, I must truthfully admit that the dancing bears in Atlantis, and the UFO in the next-to-the-last chapter, came to me later).

What this book has done is enable me to write concepts in which I believe, but for which I have no solid backing. It is, in fact, quite a sophisticated story. I suspect that parents will be stealing it from their children to read, themselves. I myself am nearly eighty-six now, and I enjoy it much more than I would have when I was Donny, in the story.

I hope you do, too. And maybe you'll have a chance to go someday to the scene of the story. If you do, please write and tell me whether you found that ruined laboratory!

THE TIME TUNNEL

CHAPTER 1

An Outing in a Transylvanian Forest

ONNY AND BOBBY WERE TWO AMERICAN children, born in Romania because their father worked there for an American oil company. They lived in a small community named Teleajen, near the town of Ploeşti, and often vacationed in a very tiny village named Timiş, in the remote Carpathian mountains of Transylvania between the towns of Predeal and Braşov.

So far this story is true. Is the rest of it? I'd like to think so, and if you'd prefer to think so, too, why don't we both just pretend that it is?

In 1935, late in the month of June, Donny and Bobby were at Timiş, vacationing. Donny was nine years old; Bobby was seven, though he'd have insisted very loudly and firmly that his *real* age was "seven *and a half!*" They were staying at the Weidis', an inn where the conditions were somewhat primitive (they had to bathe out of tin pans on wooden washstands; warm water was brought up from the kitchen). But the honey was more delicious than any you've ever tasted.

The two boys hadn't much to do. In fact, let's face it, they hadn't *anything* to do!—except run wild, play, eat honey, and— here is the important part: explore!

The high mountains around them were more or less of a wilderness: dense forests; steep slopes; unpolluted streams; miles and miles where nobody lived at all.

The boys were out exploring one morning, and went deep into the forest above the Weidi inn. They emerged all of a sudden onto a clearing, and saw before them a steep cliff. Did they climb the cliff? I'm sorry—I hope you won't blame them!—but they didn't feel quite safe with heights. So they didn't climb the cliff, but walked along the bottom of it. They'd gone some distance, when they came unexpectedly upon a ruin—and not such a very old ruin, either. It was made of both ordinary stone and shiny marble. They entered it, and found what must at one time have been some sort of science laboratory. A few crucibles and other items used in chemistry experiments were still sitting on worktables, or lay tumbled about on the floor.

What made the ruin seem fairly recent was that it was only lightly overgrown with vegetation. Many plants grew outside, making the building difficult to approach, but once the boys got inside they saw just a few plants growing out through cracks in the walls and floors. They decided the whole place looked as if an explosion had reduced the structure to its present state of utter disrepair.

"Do you think we ought to report it to someone?" Bobby asked.

"I think we should inquire carefully, first," Donny replied, "to see if anyone knows what this place was. Besides, this is, after all, an *adventure*! Once we'd reported it, it would become official, and then general, and finally, common *ordinary* knowledge!"

Bobby added, "The officials probably know all about it already anyway. They just weren't interested in a mere ruin."

"Let's go deeper inside," said Donny. "We might find something of interest."

And so, in they went, stepping over the stones and blocks of marble that lay scattered everywhere, owing evidently to the explosion. There wasn't much else: a few file cabinets, one of which was tilted against a wall, with one drawer slightly open. There were also a few work shelves and benches. The tilted cabinet with the open drawer seemed to have been broken open by the explosion, leaning as it did. Inside the open drawer, they found a file containing a few yellowed pages written in German. German was a language which, besides English, the boys spoke fairly well, as their nurses and governesses had been Austrian. The boys also had many Austrian and German friends. Still, they couldn't understand the first papers they came upon.

"Look!" cried Donny. "There's a room beyond this one. Let's see what's in there."

The back room was not very big, and was quite empty. When the boys entered it they saw a large hole in the back wall: big enough for people to walk into.

"It seems," said Bobby, "as if the hole was the main reason for this room."

"At least," Donny agreed, "it doesn't seem to have served any other purpose. Let's see what's in there."

They started to enter the hole, which they found to be a sort of tunnel leading gently downward. Entering it, they soon found themselves in darkness.

"I don't like this!" Bobby cried. "I think we'd better go back to the inn. We can come back tomorrow with a candle."

"And with something a little warmer to wear," commented Donny, shivering. "Meanwhile, we can ask what this ruin is all about—*why* it's a ruin; *what* it was used for; *who* built it."

And so they came back out, and soon were running back to the inn, to their mother, and to supper. The sun was low in the sky when they returned, and, in that deep valley, was already hidden behind the high surrounding mountains.

CHAPTER 2

The Mystery Deepens

"RAU WEIDI," DONNY ASKED THE PROPRIETRESS of the inn the next morning, "do you know anything about a ruin in the forest?"

"A ruin?" the middle-aged woman answered in German, with a motherly smile. "No, there can be no ruins. The forest around here contains no homes, and certainly no ruins."

"What we saw isn't a home. More like a science laboratory. And it's definitely a ruin."

"There can be no such thing there," Frau Weidi answered firmly. "There has never been anything like that around here. Perhaps what you saw was an old barn."

Donny said nothing. An old man seated near them in the reception room followed Donny outside afterward, and said to him, "Have you heard of Count Dracula?"

"Dracula means 'devil' in Romanian," Donny replied. "But I've never heard of a person of that name."

"Yes, I know the meaning of the word," said the old man, "though I am not Romanian, but German. However, in the last century an Austrian scientist moved into this area, and tried to frighten people with tales of a human vampire out there in the forest. No such thing existed, of course, but I heard it rumored that he invented this tale to keep people away from some work he was doing."

5

"Why could he have wanted that?" Donny asked, intrigued.

"He was a scientist," the old man replied, "and wanted to conduct some very 'hush-hush' experiments. Later, I heard that a son of his had joined him in his work. And when the father died, his son continued the project. They both shunned contact with neighbors. I only met the father once, when I was out walking in the forest. He came running out of a group of trees, shouting that I must leave that area, as he was conducting scientific experiments which might be dangerous to human life. Well, I only wanted a quiet stroll through the woods; I certainly didn't want to get blown to bits by any chemistry experiment! So I turned away and continued my walk in another direction. Later on, I asked a few people if they knew anything about that experiment, but nobody knew anything at all."

"Was that many years ago?" Donny asked.

"Well, yes, quite a few—maybe fifty years or so."

Donny thanked him, then turned away and went off to find Bobby.

"Bobby!" he cried when they met. "That ruin! Maybe it's as unknown to all the people around here as it is to Frau Weidi!"

"Oh, *great*! That means maybe we won't have to say anything about it to anyone!"

"Tomorrow Mother wants to take us to Brașov for shopping. But the day after!" Bobby was jumping up and down with excitement.

"The day after!" he cried enthusiastically.

CHAPTER 3

The Plot Thickens

HE DAY AFTER NEXT, DONNY AND BOBBY WERE VERY mysterious about their plans. Approaching Frau Weidi, Donny asked her (making an effort to hide his excitement, and, of course, speaking to her in German), "Could Bobby and I have some sandwiches to take with us? We don't plan to be here for lunch."

"And where do you intend to go?" asked Frau Weidi—also speaking, of course, in German; but I don't need to tell *you* that; you very well know that people don't speak English *everywhere*!

"Oh," replied Donny, looking nonchalantly out the window, "we just want to go a little distance into the woods. There's a brook near here, and we thought we might find a place to go swimming." (And, he thought, it really *is* a "very little distance" compared to going by car all the way to Brașov. And—he continued this thought—we *can* stop for a quick swim in the brook. Donny was a truthful child, and always weighed his words carefully to make sure he wasn't telling an untruth—even if his *full* meaning didn't always get across to others! After all, grown-ups had their own realities, usually very different ones.)

So he got his little bag of sandwiches, and the two boys, a candle in Donny's pocket, set off on their adventure. They waded across the brook toward the deep forest. (Would wading, Donny asked himself, count as swimming? Well, they could have a real swim on their way back! For the present, of course, they were much too impatient to waste even a few minutes.)

Deep into the forest they went. The sun had risen appreciably high in the sky before they reached the cliff face, and, walking beneath it, reached the old ruin.

"It really looks," Donny exclaimed, "as though no one has been here for years and years!"

"I bet," Bobby agreed, "that it's been years and years *and years*!"

"I told you about that old man I met. He said he'd met the scientist fifty years ago!"

"Gee!" exclaimed Bobby. "That sounds like before the flood they told us about in church!"

"An-te-dil-u-vian," Donny pronounced slowly with a great effort. "That's a word I remember hearing."

"Gee! What a *useless* word!" exclaimed Bobby. "But *fifty years*! I don't think I'll *ever* grow that old!"

They entered the ruin surreptitiously, as if going into a secret shrine. Silence reigned, of course, but the feeling of devastation was heightened by the fact that they now knew something of the laboratory's history.

"I wonder if this explosion happened while the old man was still alive," Donny said.

"And if it did," Bobby wondered, "was either he or his son here when it happened?"

"If either of them was alive, why is it still a ruin? It seems to me they've either deserted their project, or, . . ." (he looked at Bobby with alarm) "do you suppose they might have been killed by whoever—or *whatever*," he added fearfully—"exploded the lab?"

"You mean," said Bobby, trembling a little, "it was *meant* to be kept a secret? Do you suppose we may be in danger?"

"Well," Donny responded, "whatever it's all about, there's no guard posted here. And it wouldn't be worth posting one here now anyway, guarding nothing."

"I guess you're right," said Bobby. "But. . . ." He took a deep breath, then smiled bravely. "Gosh! that makes this *even more* of an adventure!"

Donny answered cautiously, "Yes, as long as we're safe!"

"Let's go inside," said Bobby.

They entered the main room. The tilted file cabinet attracted their attention.

"First," said Donny, "Let's see if this file folder contains any clues we can understand." They fully pulled out the half-open drawer, and removed a folder stuffed with papers. Going through them, they came upon one that seemed at least a little comprehensible. Donny said:

"Listen! This paper says, *'Der Zeit ist ein tiefes, kosmisches Geheimnis.'* 'Time is a deep cosmic secret!' *'Niemand weiss was sie bedeutet!'* 'No one knows what it means!' *'Wir müssen versuchen dieses Geheimnis zu lüften!'* 'We must try to solve this secret!' Gosh, do you suppose *that* was the purpose for this laboratory, and the reason why they kept it a secret?"

"Maybe," Bobby hazarded. "Could *that* be why they were killed?"

"Well," answered his brother, "we don't know if they really *were* killed. But someone certainly seems to have had a reason for destroying this place!"

"What could the reason have been?" Bobby wondered.

"In fact, why all the secrecy?" asked Donny.

"Yes," Bobby affirmed. "Time—I mean, we have clocks and watches to tell us the time. What's so mysterious about that?"

"Maybe," Donny reflected, "they were working on a new

kind of timepiece—one which would revolutionize normal instruments."

"But how revolutionary could that be?" asked Bobby. "I mean, something important enough to be hidden so far out in these woods?"

"I agree," said Donny. "It doesn't make sense. At least, not to me!"

They went outside and sat on a broken wall. Idly, they glanced out into the woods.

"Look!" cried Bobby suddenly. "Isn't there something over there? Let's go look."

The boys ran over to what proved to be the remains of some huge creature, lying across many bushes near the clearing.

"My Gosh!" Donny cried. "It's a *huge skeleton!*"

"It looks," shouted Bobby, "like something I saw in a book of Daddy's. It's a *dinosaur!*"

"But dinosaurs lived millions of years ago!" Donny objected. "What's a skeleton of one doing out here, deep in the forests of Transylvania? Do you suppose it might have got here alive? I mean, in recent years?"

"Impossible!" Bobby answered. He then paused, and cried, "Look! There's some flesh on those bones! Most of it has been eaten, but the monster can't have died all that long ago!"

Donny paused a moment, then said, "Yes, well I guess nearly fifty years would be recent compared to *millions* of years!" He paused a moment, reflecting. Then, "Holy smoke, Bobby! Do you suppose those remarks about time didn't mean *our* time—clocks, watches, and things—but another kind of time altogether?"

Bobby pulled on his arm. "Let's go back and look in those files. Maybe they'll tell us something we need to know."

They raced back to the building, and—first setting their sandwich bag upon a worktable—looked further through the files in the still-open drawer. They soon found a file folder labeled, "*Amerikanische Forschung.*"

"I don't know what *Forschung* means," said Donny, "but we both know that Amerikanische means 'American.' Let's look inside."

They opened the file. There, on the very first page they found, was the English translation: "American Research." With eager fingers they pulled out a sheaf of papers and read:

"Summary of what follows: Time does not go as people think, in a straight line from past to present to future. Rather, it proceeds in a circle around a center in the eternal *NOW*. Time is, basically, an illusion. Whatever was in the past not only *was*, but is now, and will be, forever. Whatever happens doesn't really happen at all, except as a mental concept. If one could divorce himself from passing time altogether and reduce his sense of selfhood to absolute zero, he would be able to appear again at any specific time, whether in the past or in the future."

"Gosh!" exclaimed Donny. "It doesn't make any sense to me at all, but if that dinosaur out there was brought here from another time zone, I can see how this laboratory needed to be kept a secret. What those two scientists were doing here seems to me more explosive than dynamite!"

"Why would that be?" Bobby asked,

"Well, don't you see? If anyone could bring that huge dinosaur forward in time, what might they not have been able to bring back from the future? If they could go back in time, they had to be able to go forward, too, and bring things back from that time zone to our own. What if man, violent as so many people are today, were confronted with high technology brought back from the future? He might be able in a flash to destroy entire nations—what then? Mankind isn't ready for such knowledge! Someone might destroy the whole planet just because he hadn't learned to control his own emotions!"

Bobby took a deep breath. "Wow! What if a child our age . . ." (seeing Donny's smiling expression) "well, gee, anyone very young: what if he were allowed to play with a real gun? Even that would be like dynamite!"

Donny, exhaling as if to blow out the breath Bobby had just inhaled, exclaimed, "Do you suppose that hole in the back room led to a time tunnel?"

"If we're very careful, do we dare to find out?" Bobby asked.

Fateful words! Much was to depend on Donny's answer.

"Let's give it a try!" Donny cried.

CHAPTER 4

A First Step

**T**HEY ENTERED THE TUNNEL. THE FIRST THING they noticed as they got deeper inside was a low humming sound, coming in rhythmic pulses from below them (especially from below, it seemed) and from all around.

Donny's expression (there was a slowly growing light inside the tunnel for his expression to be visible) revealed puzzlement.

"How can there be that hum? In this ruin there *can't* be any electricity."

"I doubt that there was ever any electricity here," commented Bobby, "even *before* this place became a ruin. I mean, way out here in this primitive . . . ?"

"'*Pristine*,' I think, is the word . . ."

"Okay, pristine forest," corrected Bobby, willing to accommodate his brother.

"Or maybe '*primeval*'? I read that somewhere in a book."

"Okay," said Bobby. "Whatever. What a big one you are for words!"

"Well, but the point is, where can that pulsing sound be coming from?"

"It reminds me a bit of the engine of a huge ocean liner," cried Bobby. They had already crossed the Atlantic by ship more than once.

"You're right!" Donny answered. "On a ship, you can hear that sound everywhere!"

"Except that this sound seems almost alive!" continued Bobby.

"Do you notice something else? The further we walk into this tunnel, the more it keeps shrinking!"

Bobby cried out fearfully, "And *we're* shrinking with it! Oh! Let's get out of here!"

They tried to turn back. "I can't!" Donny cried.

"Neither can I!" whispered Bobby. The pulsing sound seemed to be forcing them forward. What could they do? Terror-stricken, they joined hands for mutual protection.

Well, dear Reader, what would *you* have done in their place? Maybe practice would have made you perfect, but this, remember, was their first experience of the tunnel. Frankly, I think *I'd* have been scared out of my wits! And I'd have clung to the hand of the nearest, largest, *toughest* grown-up I could find! Yet poor Donny and Bobby were only children: Donny was nine; Bobby was seven—well, all right, seven and a *full half!*

Death didn't seem to threaten them, however. Both the tunnel and their own bodies kept on shrinking, but their *consciousness* remained unchanged. The light, at least, was now growing stronger. It seemed to be coming from some source other than daylight. A speck of dust floated by them: it looked like a huge boulder! And they themselves kept shrinking!

What had been a mere hint of condensation on the floor became a puddle, then a pond, then a lake. And they themselves were *in* that lake! Soon, they beheld huge monsters floating in the water all around them.

"They look like paramecia!" Donny cried. "I once saw some through a microscope in a pre-science class."

Bobby shouted, "Look at those whirling lights around us! They look like the pictures of atoms I saw in a book last week!"

Donny cried, "And even they keep growing bigger!"

"My gosh!" Bobby cried excitedly. "They look like suns and planets and moons!"

"And *still* we're shrinking!"

"Is this good—or is it *terrible*!? We keep shrinking, but still we remain ourselves!"

"We no longer seem to have bodies," cried Donny, "but we're still conscious!"

"*More* conscious!" Bobby cried. "I not only see everything more clearly, but I'm even *more* aware of everything around me!"

"Oh, God!" cried Donny, "my body seems to have shrunk to nothing! What *is* this! What's that large zero forming around us?"

All of a sudden they emerged from the tunnel. That large zero had become a sphere of light; it surrounded them like a luminescent bubble, outside of which they saw a countryside of trees, flowers, and great natural beauty.

"Where *are* we?" cried Bobby.

"Remember what we read in that file folder?" Donny answered. "The summary, as I still remember it, went something like this: 'If one could divorce himself from passing time and reduce his sense of selfhood to absolute zero, he would find it possible to appear again at any specific time, whether in time past or in future time.'"

"My gosh!" Bobby exclaimed. "Then this light around us *is* that zero!"

"Is this scene," Donny cried, "some sort of border zone between past and future? We must be *out of time* altogether, as we know it!"

Bobby started to cry. "How will we ever get back to the inn?

And we left those sandwiches on the worktable!" He began to shiver. "We'll starve to death!"

Consolingly Donny said, "Well, if we're out of time, maybe we're past getting hungry, too."

Bobby suddenly stopped sobbing. "Look!" he cried. "Over there! There's someone on the ground!"

They thought themselves in that direction, and to their astonishment the sphere moved with that thought!

"It's a man!" cried Donny. Whoever it was seemed to be asleep.

"Hey!" Bobby shouted. "Wake up!" The man didn't move. They stared at him a moment in silence. "Are you dead? Are you like that dinosaur out there?"

The man stirred. "Dinosaur?" he muttered as if vaguely remembering the word.

"Yes, dinosaur!" shouted Donny.

"You mean, you actually *saw* the dinosaur?" asked the man, opening his eyes and rising to a sitting position in sudden panic, though still he spoke vaguely.

"Yes," cried Bobby. "Out there, beyond the tunnel."

"You—you *found* the tunnel?"

"Of course," said Bobby.

The man's head seemed to be clearing. "I'm starting to remember! But the dinosaur! You said it's on the other side?! Oh! Oh! how—how *TERRIBLE!*"

"No!" said Donny. "Not terrible. It's dead."

"Dead! Is it really dead? Oh, *thank God*!" the man cried out emotionally, then began to laugh almost hysterically. "I was afraid it would still be alive, and creating havoc."

"But how did it ever get there?" urged Bobby.

The man's head seemed to clear completely. "Yes! It's

understandable to me now. But first, we've got to get you out of your time-light sphere. As long as you're in it, you'll be visible only to me, because I too came out of that tunnel. No one will be able to hear you. You'll watch others, but no one will know you're there, watching them!"

Donny then asked, "So how do we get out of this sphere?"

"It's easy enough. The light composing it is a vibration of energy. You can bring that light up around you, or remove it altogether, by first realizing that the energy in your hands, combined with the power of breath, with focused concentration, and with will power, can either dissolve the sphere or re-create it.

"The time-light sphere formed around you when you were reduced to zero. You must have been holding hands—believe me, I know how frightened you must have been! I was scared too, the first time—and that's why only one sphere formed around the two of you, instead of your being in two separate spheres. The sphere formed because zero ego-consciousness, as opposed to what lies after that, emerges naturally into a sphere of light.

"But now what you need to do is stand up straight in that sphere."

The boys stood as close to the center of the sphere as they could.

"Now, raise your hands high above your heads." The boys did as directed.

"Next, inhale with a deep breath, and feel that you are inhaling pure energy." The boys did that, too.

"Then send as much energy to your hands as you can." Again, the boys followed directions.

"Now! Bring your hands and arms downward, keeping the arms straight out to your sides as if outlining the shape of your time-light sphere. As you do so, exhale as if dispersing the energy into that sphere from your fingertips."

The boys did this, too. To their amazement, they saw the light around them disappear in a downward-rolling scroll. When their arms touched their thighs, the sphere had disappeared!

"You see how simple it is?" the man said. "Now, when you want to create that sphere around you again, or to create *two* spheres (since there are two of you), all you have to do is this: Lower your arms to your sides; think energy; then fill your hands with energy. Keep your will power and concentration very focused, and bring your hands up and out to the side in an arc, holding your arms straight out all the time until the two hands touch each other above the head.

"First, however, do this: Tense, then relax, exhaling, and think of yourselves as exhaling any remaining tension from your bodies. Then inhale, and slowly fill yourselves not only with air, but with energy—energy, and light."

The boys did so, and found the "scroll" of light rising up again around their bodies—becoming this time, however, *two* spheres of light.

"These time-light spheres are very important. They will keep you invisible to others, and also inaudible. Inaudible," he explained, "means 'impossible to be heard.' And the spheres will protect you from anything that may be going on around you."

Bobby returned to a thought that persisted in his mind. "How did that dinosaur get there?"

"Yes," answered the man. "That was your question! But before I answer you let me back up a little:

"What happened was this. Shortly before my father died, he warned me, 'We've always traveled together, but soon now you'll have to travel alone. It's important for you to remember this truth: When time traveling—it's essential that you NOT *go too fast*!

"'Whether going backward or forward in time, be sure to go *gently*. There won't be any trouble, then. But if you—well,' he paused then, 'do you remember that time when we went forward in this century, and saw a fighter plane soar up into the sky?'

"I told him I remembered it, and added, 'There was a sudden explosion.'

"'Yes,' said my father, confirming that this was just what he was talking about. 'What the plane had just done was break through what we later heard described as the *"sound barrier."* Well, you smiled at the time, and thought the word quaint. But I warned you: There's also something we might call the *time barrier*, and this barrier isn't quaint at all! If you go through time in either direction, whether past or future, but move too fast, you will break through that time barrier. What will happen then— in our own time zone—is that there will be an explosion. I don't know how big the explosion will be, but, like all explosions, its effect will be unpleasant—in fact, it might be terrific!'

"After my father died," the younger man continued, "I took to experimenting. Somehow I became fascinated with that era millions of years ago, when dinosaurs roamed the earth. I wondered what they looked like, how they behaved, if they were completely stupid or perhaps more intelligent than paleontologists have made them out to be from the small size of their brains relative to their bodies. I wondered if the meat-eaters among them, like the Tyrannosaurus Rex, were randomly vicious, or if they killed only to eat. Anyway—I wondered!

"One day, I found myself in my time-light sphere, roaming above a tropical plain where I saw many huge reptiles, some of them around a large lake, wallowing in deep mud; some were grazing in nearby grass; some were flying through the air. None of them could see me, and I knew I was completely safe.

"A crazy impulse then seized me: I decided to *ride* one of those huge monsters! 'If any threat appears,' I told myself, 'I can always escape to safety in a different time zone.' So I removed my protective time-light sphere, as I've taught you to do, and approached a huge monster from behind. I clambered up its back, finding its scales to be so thick that the creature didn't even notice me! It was fun, too, riding so high up, surveying the terrain around me. We must have spent a good hour that way when suddenly a Tyrannosaurus Rex, with a terrific roar, came charging at us from behind. It was bent on killing my ride. As for me, I don't think it even saw me! I imagine that, to that huge monster, I was little bigger than an ant.

"Well, there was one thing I hadn't learned yet about time travel, and that's if you are holding anything in your hand, or grasping it with your knees as I'd been doing, it comes *with you* when you leave that time zone! In escaping the Tyrannosaurus Rex, I was thinking only of saving myself. And I was in such a desperate hurry to escape that I left that zone too quickly.

"Well, I'm sure you've guessed what happened: I broke through the time barrier! There ensued a tremendous explosion. Because time doesn't actually *pass* in this timeless, mind-only zone we're now in, I was hurled back to the present point of entry into it. The creature I was riding got thrown *forward*, and I got thrown *backward*. The dinosaur went through the tunnel, and I got hurled back into this timelessness zone. I was still without my protective sphere of light, from which I'd emerged to ride the monster. And I just lay here on the ground, bereft of energy, completely exhausted."

Donny then asked, "But how did the huge dinosaur get through that narrow tunnel?"

"Why, don't you remember?" said the man. "It lost its size on entering the tunnel! Physically speaking, it became zero. As it emerged on the other side, it resumed its own shape and size. As for me, I lost all consciousness. And because time on this side doesn't pass—we're always in the timeless NOW—I may have been lying here for hours, days, weeks, months—even *years*! What year is it in your time zone, anyway?"

"Nineteen thirty-five," Donny informed him.

"Good heavens! and I left on my voyage in September, nineteen-*thirty*! That means five years have passed in your time, but here, where time doesn't exist, it's as though I had returned only moments ago!"

"How can that be?" Bobby asked.

"Well," replied the man, "when you dream, isn't time mental also? You might dream that a hundred years pass by in just a few minutes—even in mere seconds of your so-called 'normal' time. It's even more true in this zone, for there's a consistency here that isn't found in dreams. In dreams, you can be on a beach at sea level, and suddenly the sand becomes snow, and you're struggling to get it out of your eyes to see your way through dense fog as you struggle to reach a mountaintop. And then all of a sudden the thought of snow brings you, let us say, to soap bubbles, and there you are, seated in your bathtub, getting lathered by your mother!"

Donny, after thinking this through for a moment, finally said, "Then if, while five years passed in our own zone, no time passed here, what happens if time does pass here? Does that mean that even more time passes there, or less, or none at all? As you can see, I'm confused."

The man smiled. "I told you, time here is only a mental concept. I went back millions of years on that 'outing,' and yet I came back to my own year—virtually to the same moment as when I'd left. Everything on this side is NOW. But *now*, too, is based simply on the fact that we're conscious, and consciousness is always *now*, in the present tense. The present is, in fact, the only real time there is. Everything else is only movement in that never-moving reality—like waves on the surface of a sea, the over-all level of which never changes."

At this, Bobby cried, "This is all much too much for me!" He paused a moment, then continued: "Okay, so yesterday we both went to Brașov. Suppose we went back there now. We'd be here, and we'd be also there. We'd be *there then*, but we'd be *here now*. Who, really, would be anywhere at all?"

"You'd be here, in the only final reality there is: NOW. They wouldn't be there, because their *permanent* reality would remain *here*. You'd be riding a wave called 'then,' but from *here* you'd see that wave as a mere distortion of *now*. From here, you couldn't also be there. Others would see you, but you wouldn't see yourself. And since both of you are here *together*, your view there of each other would be sort of muffled."

"I just don't understand at all what you're talking about!" lamented Bobby.

"Shall we try it?"

"Why not?" cried Donny.

"All right, then, let's re-create our time-light spheres so we can't be seen."

They did so. Then Donny and Bobby thought the three of them back to the day before, when he and his brother had been sitting in the car, waiting outside the shop their mother had just entered. Their new friend was with them, observing the scene from his own time-light bubble, but of course he could only view everything from the outside. The odd thing, for the boys, was that they didn't see or hear themselves in that car!

Instead, because they were *here* in their time-light spheres, they saw only two vaguely transparent mists. Otherwise, the places they'd occupied looked empty! And all they heard of their own voices in the car was a sort of mumble.

Their mother came out of the shop, carrying a bag of things to eat.

"I've brought you some *Apfelstrudel*, boys, with *Schlag*. We'll have it tomorrow night at dinner." There ensued a dull mumble. Their mother then spoke again, as if answering a question: "*Schlag* is a word for whipped cream, Bobby." A mumble, and then, "Yes, it's sweetened, and put on the *Strudel*." Another mumble, then: "*Strudel*, Bobby, is a kind of dessert. It really means 'vortex,' or 'whirlpool,' but in this case the pastry is made of many thin layers folded around their apple at the center." This time the mumble held an extra note of enthusiasm. Then again she said: "All right, boys, just enjoy the ride. I must think about something I have to do tomorrow."

The car took off. The boys' seats still seemed to hold only transparent mists.

"Weird!" Bobby commented from his own time-light sphere. And weird it certainly was!

"And so you see," their new friend said as they found themselves suddenly back where they'd been. They removed their protective envelopes, and sat down again on the grass. "And so you see," he repeated, "your true self, your *consciousness* of self, is always here, and always *now*. It simply can't be here and now, and also there and then, at the same time. You always see yourselves from the inside, not from without. That is why your figures in the car looked filmy and transparent. Bobby's physical reality, for Donny, was dimmed because Bobby could see himself only from inside himself. And Donny's physical reality, for Bobby, was dimmed by the fact that Donny saw everything from inside *himself*."

Donny suddenly sat up. "I think we'd better get back! It's getting late." As the boys rose to their feet, their new friend remarked wryly, "It may be earlier than you think!"

"We'd better rush home, anyway," Donny replied. "I don't want to miss that Apfelstrudel for supper!"

"With Schlag!" enthused Bobby.

They ran toward the clump of bushes, behind which the entrance to the tunnel awaited them. And then, suddenly: the same experience came in reverse! Their zero body-sizes became, first, two clouds of atoms; then were immersed in a lake full of paramecia; then were trying to avoid huge boulders of dust; then all at once, they became tiny human forms first, and then—well, you know the rest: Suddenly, they were little boys again!

Snatching up their bag of sandwiches from the lab table, they ran out into the sunlight, and kept right on running toward the inn.

"That's funny," said Donny. "The sun looks about as high as it was when we entered that ruin!"

"Gee," commented Bobby. "It *ought* to be getting on for twilight!"

"Let's look for a place in the brook where we can swim!" shouted Donny. "We *told* Frau Weidi, remember, that we'd have a swim today?"

"Right! This way we can truthfully say that we did go swimming."

On reaching the brook, they walked up and down the bank until they found a place where the water was deep enough for a good dip. Throwing off their clothes, they jumped into the water and played in it for a few minutes. Then, emerging, they dressed and headed for home. Donny remarked:

"Well, at least we kept our word!"

But Bobby said, "I think if we eat our sandwiches right now, we won't spoil our appetites for supper!"

"And for those Apfelstrudels."

"With *Schlag*!" added Bobby.

They ate their sandwiches, and arrived at the inn in plenty of time for supper.

"Did you enjoy your swim?" Frau Weidi asked them with a motherly smile.

"More than you'll ever know!" cried Donny enthusiastically.

"It *is* getting hot!" Frau Weidi rejoined. "I wish I could take time off and rest a little, with no thought of what is next in my life, and what may have been left undone today, or what I accomplished yesterday."

The boys looked at each other with meaning smiles, then went quietly up to their room.

CHAPTER 5

Back Again!

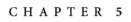

HE NEXT DAY THEY EMERGED ONCE MORE FROM the tunnel, encased in their bubbles of light. This time, however, they came through calmly and without a tremor of fear. Their new friend was there waiting for them. Once they'd dissolved their time-light spheres, they greeted him.

"Have we been gone long?" Bobby asked.

"Only a minute or two," answered their new friend. "I wasn't bored!"

Donny apologized, "I'm sorry, but so much happened yesterday, we forgot to ask you your name."

"I'm Hansel," replied the young man. "It sounds more friendly than Hans." With a smile, he extended a hand to each of them.

"And where did you learn such good English, Hansel?" asked Donny.

"In America. I spent two years there with my father, and went to school there."

Bobby said politely, "I wish we'd been able to meet your father!"

Hansel said, "Well, why not? We can go back there right now, if you like. When we get there, we can dissolve our time-light spheres."

"Oh, *let's* do it!" cried Bobby. "Maybe he can tell us himself why he put out that story about Dracula!"

"Oh, you heard that story, did you?" Hansel replied with a smile. "Papa never talked much about it, even to me. But of course we can go back right now to the time when he was still alive."

They enclosed themselves in their spheres of light. Hansel, this time, did the wishing. Soon they found themselves back in his father's time. There before them stood an old man, sporting a large white mustache and longish white hair. Quickly they dissolved their time-light spheres so as to be visible to him. The old man greeted them with a welcoming smile.

"*Ach*, Hansel, *ich freue mich sehr dich zu zehen!*"

"Yes, Papa. I'm so happy to see you, too. But let's speak in English now. My two friends here are American. Oh, how wonderful it is to see you, Papa!" The two men embraced lovingly. "I have amazing things to tell you. But first let me introduce my friends. This is Donny; he's nine years old. And this is his brother Bobby, seven."

"Seven and a *half*," corrected Bobby a little indignantly, straightening himself slightly.

"Sorry, seven *and a half*." Hansel smiled, amused at this correction. To his father he continued, "They found our laboratory, and the time tunnel. And they've brought news. They also asked me a question that only you can answer, Papa; that's why we're here." Hansel then looked sad. "Papa, our laboratory has been destroyed!"

"Destroyed!" exclaimed the old man, speaking in a thick German accent. "But *vy*? *How?*" For a moment he looked sad. "Ess vas such a vonderful vorkplace!"

"I know, Papa. I'm afraid I did just what you told me *not* to do! I broke through the time barrier."

"You *did*? But how terrible! Well, at least you surfifed; das ist der main sing. Vot happened?"

"I was escaping an attack by a huge Tyrannosaurus Rex in the Mesozoic Era. In my haste, I forgot what you'd told me, and escaped too quickly."

"But at least se time tunnel ist shtill zer, und it vorks! Osservise zees boys vould not be here mit us."

"Yes, Papa, but things happened. Oh, did they *ever* happen!"

"Vas ist's dat you mean?"

"Well, I was riding on another dinosaur . . ."—his father looked quite shocked—"and, because I was gripping it with my legs, it came back with me."

"Gott im Himmel! Und so der ess ist, raffaging ze whole countryside!"

"No, no Papa! No! The explosion killed it. It was thrown forward, *into* time. And I was thrown backward, *out of* time. But these boys have brought the news that the lab is in ruins. I'm so sorry."

"Ach! vy should ve grief? Ess ist no longer my vorry! Don't let it be yours."

"Sir," said Donny, "we'd like to know something about Dracula!"

"Dracula!" answered the old man. "But I know nossing about Dracula. Er ist only a myth."

"I know. But another old man"—then, politely—"forgive me, Sir; I know you're not really old."

The old man smiled. "I haff no age! but go on. I know vas you mean."

"Well, this old man I met told me you yourself invented that myth to protect that area around your laboratory. What I want to know is, What *is* that myth? I've never heard it."

The old man smiled again. "Ach, es ist only silly! Maybe you haffen't heard, but vampires ist ein species of bat in Sout America vhich socks blutt—excuse please, blood." (He pronounced this word to rhyme with *mood*.) "I pretended zer liffed a *human* vampire out zer in se Transylvanian forest."

"But is there any basis for that myth?"

"Vell, zer liffed long ago a ruler in Romania—centuries before your time—who impaled many peoples sroo se heart mitt vooden shtakes. His name vass Vlad, und zey called him Dracula, meaning Vlad ze devil. So I used zat myth to invent a *man* called Dracula. I turned his act of impaling people into a blutt-sucking fiend! And he himself could be killt only by a shtake driffen sroo se heart. I shpoke in fun, of course, but my purpose wass at the same time serious. I needed to discourage people from coming anywhere near our vorkplace."

Bobby piped up, "Wouldn't it be fun just to have a peep at that creep, Vlad!"

Hansel chimed in, "We could go back, if you like, to the time when Vlad lived. It must have been a terrible period!"

Donny asked the old man, "Would you like to come, Sir? Or would it be too painful to see the actual beginning of the Dracula story?"

"Ach! vy should I grief? Ess ist no longer my vorry!" said the father, repeating the statement he'd made earlier. "Neizer ist ess your vorry, in zis present dream time. I sink my real ego ist enchoying a much besser place! No, you go. I don't really shtay here, eiser. I shtay in zat ozzer, besser place."

Accordingly, they went without him, back to the time of Vlad. Moments later, they emerged onto a large, flat plain where thousands of bodies lay spread out, spread-eagled on the ground, stakes protruding from their chests. They'd been impaled through the heart. Prisoners were huddled in a large group at the edge of the field. They obviously desired desperately to avoid the dreadful fate that awaited them. Armed soldiers stood nearby, laughing brutally, while Vlad himself, a vicious-looking specimen of humanity, stood on a platform, gazing down fiercely on the spectacle, a cruel smile hiding, masklike, any genuine sentiments he may have felt. He was laughing sadistically. Several solders held a struggling prisoner spread-eagled on the ground, four of them stretching out his legs and arms. The fifth was just in the act of plunging a stake into the prisoner's heart. Other prisoners moaned as they watched this fearful spectacle.

Donny shuddered. Covering his eyes, he looked away. "Oh it's too *horrible*! Isn't there something we can do to stop this terrible carnage?"

Bobby wept, "I wish we could just wipe the whole scene out of existence!"

"I'm afraid you can't do that," said Hansel.

"Why not?" cried the boys simultaneously.

"This was the way people were dreaming in those days," replied Hansel. "Kings had absolute power, and the peasants had no power at all. To the rulers, peasants were no more than cattle."

"But why didn't they rebel?" Bobby asked.

"After centuries, they finally did—not here in Romania, but later on, in France. A very bloody revolution broke out there, near the end of the eighteenth century. Huge numbers of aristocrats, including even the king and queen, died beneath the guillotine."

"What's a ghilteen?" asked Bobby.

"A guillotine was a large blade, suspended on a larger frame. The blade descended and sliced off people's heads."

"Ugh! How terrible!" said the boys together.

"In Switzerland—earlier than the French Revolution," Hansel continued, "it was during the fourteenth or fifteenth century—the peasants won *their* freedom, too. It began with William Tell. Would you like to go see him? That's better than only reading about him."

Donny shuddered. "If what he went through was anything like what we've just seen, I think I'd rather sit this one out."

"No, this time things were very different. William was an archer, and a very good one. He was also a peasant. Gessler, his overlord, was a tyrant. Gessler put his hat on a pole and, in order to test his subjects' obedience, commanded that every man must bow to the hat when passing it.

"One day, William Tell walked proudly by it without bowing. Gessler, when this 'insult' was reported to him, called Tell before him and told him with a sneer that he would pardon Tell if he agreed to shoot an apple off his little son's head. Shall we go back and have a look?"

They thought themselves from Vlad's time to that of William Tell. Mountains towered high above them in the background. William Tell was standing by a lake, his little son some twenty yards in front of him with an apple on his head. The tyrant Gessler was standing off to one side, a little distance away. He was smiling coldly; his supporters around him were grinning in derision.

William Tell grimly strung his crossbow, pulled the string, then lowered the bow and gave Gessler an enraged look.

"My own son!" he cried.

"Yes!" Gessler frowned grimly. "Wouldn't his death be a fair price for your own freedom?"

"Monster!" muttered poor William. He then called out to his little son, "Liebling, please forgive me! You see I have no choice.

It isn't only my freedom: it's that of all our people. And if I don't shoot, he'll certainly kill us both!"

"Go ahead, Papa!" cried the little boy. "I know you won't miss." The child did tremble a bit, however!

William raised his bow again, placed the arrow against the string, pulled back, and let fly. The arrow penetrated the center of the apple. His son fell to the ground in a faint.

William Tell then quickly took out a second arrow from his quiver, turned like lightning, and shot Gessler through the heart. As Gessler fell dead to the ground, his supporters gathered around to help him. William then seized the little boy, who was conscious again by this time, and leapt with him into the boat they'd arrived in, which they'd left tied to the shore. They rowed hastily away, passing beyond the reach of Gessler's men before they could react.

"What a drama!" cried Donny. "And so what William Tell did was spark a revolution? I'm so glad. No one should be treated so cruelly."

Bobby joined in with the affirmation: "William Tell was as good as any of those other men."

"*Much better!*" cried Donny. "His courage showed that his character was truly noble, whereas Gessler showed only meanness, arrogance, and cruelty."

Hansel then said to them, "There was another episode in that revolt, showing how intelligently creative the peasants were. This happened, I think, some years later. The aristocrats came on horseback at night, in armor and full battle array. They waited in the woods for daylight before making their attack."

The boys suddenly found themselves seated with Hansel in their time-light spheres above a large field. It was nighttime, but below them they could see a large group of peasants diverting a stream toward the field, and flooding it. By morning the field had become a sheet of ice. At dawn, the knights attacked. As soon as they came out onto that icy field, their horses began slipping and falling to the ground. The knights flopped about helplessly, hampered by their heavy armor. The peasants came out onto the field with pitchforks and slew them all.

"Wow!" cried Donny. "Gruesome, but just!"

"The peasants sure showed their rulers they were no better just for being bigger, richer, and more powerful than themselves!" was Bobby's comment.

"And the rulers learned that peasants were just as human as anyone else!" said Donny.

"What do you say, now, that we go back 'home'?" said Hansel. "We've had a pretty full day of it."

"I'll say we have!" said Bobby with a little shudder.

Moments later, they found themselves back on the grass outside their tunnel. Scrolling down their light spheres, they sat down comfortably on the ground in a reminiscing mood.

"I have a question," asked Donny. "Why were those people all speaking English? That surely wasn't their language then, was it?"

"No, of course not," Hansel replied. "What you were hearing was their thoughts, not their words. And you could hear their real thoughts more truly, because people's actual words often hide what they really think."

"How can that be?" asked Bobby.

"Well, like when William Tell called Gessler a monster, I don't imagine he really said that: he only thought it. Surely he knew it would be too dangerous to voice the thought out loud."

"So the words we heard in English were really spoken in German? But what about the thoughts themselves? I agree that William Tell probably didn't *say* 'Monster!' in any language. But even in thinking it, he must have thought it in German."

"Yes, of course he did," Hansel replied. "But behind even the words we think are our *intentions*. It's those *intentions* which are the true, universal language of mankind."

Bobby spoke up eagerly. "Hansel, you said we couldn't change history. But couldn't we have gotten *others* to change it? What if we'd gone back to Vlad's time, and told the peasants there about that field the peasants iced over in Switzerland. Mightn't the Romanian peasants then have been persuaded to make war on Vlad themselves, using new, creative methods?"

"It wouldn't have been possible. You see, first of all, doing so would have opposed the way people were dreaming in those days. But also there's a power in destiny which overwhelms reason itself.

"How many times," he continued, "have *you* done something which was not reasonable—which, perhaps, wasn't even *right*— just because some impulse inside you forced you to do it?"

"Never!" cried Bobby.

"Oh yes you have!" cried Donny. "Remember just yesterday, when Mother told you not to eat too much *Schlag*, and you ate it anyway? Later you had a stomachache, didn't you?"

"Oh, if that's all you meant," Bobby replied. Then, addressing Hansel, he continued, "I thought you meant something more like, I was cruel. I've never been cruel."

"He's right," interspersed Donny. "He may be self-assertive, but I've never known him to be cruel."

"Well," Bobby protested, "what's wrong with being self-assertive? I'm as good as anyone else."

"And as *big*?" Donny asked with a sly grin.

Bobby inhaled preparatory to making a good reply, but Hansel intervened by saying: "But don't you see, you're both justifying what I said! You don't have a tendency to be cruel, Bobby, but your tendency to be self-assertive won't let you rest even when the people around you are older and obviously *know* more than you. So when you know, as you certainly must, that they know things you couldn't possibly know, you feel you somehow have to get into the act!"

"But would I *hurt* people to do that?" asked Bobby.

"I'm quite sure *you* wouldn't. But can't you see that others, in whom that tendency was stronger, might ignore the feelings of other people altogether?"

Donny spoke up then. "Then what you're saying is that some people are so self-assertive that not even reasoning with them would make them any less so?"

"Of course that's what I mean!" Hansel answered.

"Well, I can see that," Donny said, "but we were talking about individuals, whereas what we're dealing with here is the consciousness of a whole people, a *nation*, perhaps of even an entire time-period in history. *Some* people today may be as self-assertive as you say, but look at Bobby: He's an exception, certainly. So also, I like to think, am I. Neither of us is so self-assertive as to want to hurt anybody."

"In my travels through history," said Hansel, "I've come to the conclusion that mankind as a whole is sometimes more aware, and sometimes less so. I can't explain it, but history seems to rise and fall, like the ocean waves. I've noticed that, when those waves rise and fall, and as the general level of awareness descends, people keep harking back to the 'good old days.' Very few people, during such dips in consciousness, think of improving matters. And then, as the wave starts to *rise* again, people begin looking for the future to improve. They try to better themselves. Instead of thinking, 'They did things better in the old days,' they look about for better diets, better machinery, more efficient ways of doing things."

"Our Daddy's here in this country to find oil," said Donny. "He says a hundred years ago it was seeping up out of the ground, and no one knew what to do with it."

"A few years from now," continued Hansel, "smoking will be banned from public places. People today not only want, but *expect* things, and themselves also, to improve."

"I'm fascinated!" cried Donny,

"Look at the cruelty of the Roman era," Hansel continued. "Have your parents told you anything about it?"

"We've studied it in school. Two summers ago we went to Athens, and Mother and Daddy told us something about those times in history."

"Well," Hansel continued, "in the Roman Colosseum they had terrible so-called 'circus games.' Gladiators cruelly slaughtered one another. Christians were offered to the lions as entertainment for the masses. If anyone tried, for any reason at all, to offer such 'sport' today, he'd be publicly excoriated. Who today, in fact, would even dare try such a thing?"

Donny asked, "Then what's the point in wandering through history, if we can't change anything for the better? What is the use of seeing such horrors as mass slaughter and persecution?"

Hansel looked at him penetratingly. "But don't you think," he answered, "that certain scenes from history might make you ponder how you might improve *yourself?*"

"Is *that* the main benefit of time travel?"

"Well, isn't it? Reflect: Being with people helps you to see faults you don't like in others, or, for that matter, good qualities you see in others that you'd like to assume for yourself. We *need* other people; they help us to mature. So, then, think of people, as we know them basically to be, presenting various aspects of human nature through the ever-changing panorama of history.

From their examples, we can see potentials in ourselves for both improvement and degradation."

"Oh, that sounds exciting!" cried Donny. "What if we went back to the time of the pyramids, and saw what the people were like *then*!"

"We could see how they built those great monuments!" added Bobby. "Daddy said it was slave labor that built them."

"But how could anyone who used slave labor," Donny hazarded, "have been so sensitive as even to *think* of building such lofty and amazing structures?"

"I agree," Hansel said. "It seems to me that the people then must have been too highly evolved in consciousness even to *think* of keeping slaves, or of working them mercilessly just to give physical shape to their fantasies."

"Yes," Donny mused, "if the things people did then were as lofty as they seem, surely their *thoughts*, too, would have been lofty. They *can't* have been as cruel even as many people are today. The whole consciousness back then must have been higher than what it is now."

"But can people change that much from age to age?" Bobby wondered.

"As people are dreaming today," Hansel said, "it would not be possible. But roaming over history, as I've been doing for years, I've seen that people's consciousness *does* change. Why don't we go *forward* in time, later, and see what the majority of people will be like centuries from now? I've gone there somewhat, and, believe me, I can promise you a few surprises!"

"Wow!" cried Donny. "*That* would be exciting!"

Bobby interposed, returning to his first theme, "But how can anyone even *want* to own people as slaves?"

"I think it's time," said Hansel, rising to his feet, "to give this subject a rest. We've had quite enough for one day. It isn't late at the inn, but you'd better get back there now, before you are missed."

"Oh, gosh!" cried Donny. "You're right! Frau Weidi probably thinks we're still swimming and getting waterlogged!"

The boys waved their hands quickly to Hansel, then hurried off to the bushes, behind which they entered the time tunnel.

"See you tomorrow!" cried Donny.

"If we're allowed to come," added Bobby.

Emerging at the other end, Donny said, "We'd better have a swim, so we'll be telling the truth to Frau Weidi when we say that's what we've been doing."

"Look!" Bobby cried. "The sun's still high overhead!"

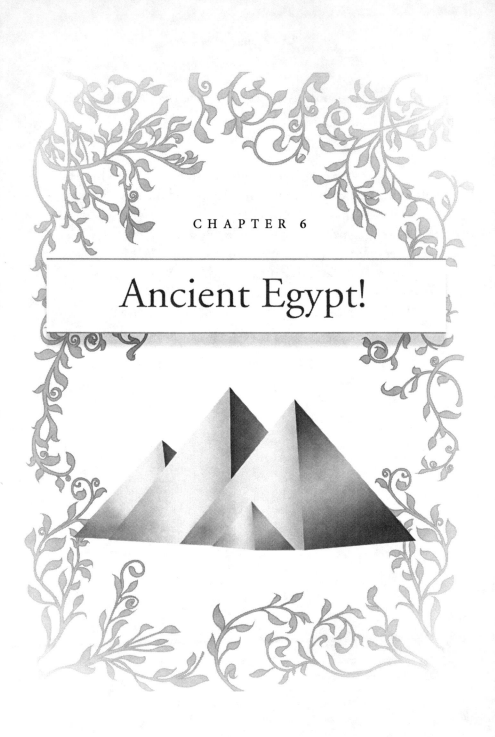

CHAPTER 6

Ancient Egypt!

HE NEXT MORNING, THE BOYS RETURNED FROM time to timelessness. Hansel was there waiting for them—patiently of course, for (as he said), "There was no delay to get impatient about."

"There's something I've been wanting to ask you," said Bobby, "and I keep forgetting to. My question is: What is that hum we hear every time we come through the time tunnel? As I remarked to Donny the first time we entered it, the hum seems almost alive!"

"It *is* alive, in a sense," answered Hansel. "You see, the 'substance' of everything is consciousness. Science doesn't know this yet, but I've discovered this truth in my travels to the future. Nowadays, scientists still insist that the only reality is what we can see and feel: things touchable, weighable, and measurable. 'Matter can neither be created nor destroyed' is the slogan they proclaim as if shouting it from the housetops. But what they don't know is that matter *can* in fact be *converted*: into energy! Some years from now they'll explode the atom and turn it into energy. And energy, in time, will be found to be only thought vibrations. More centuries later, they'll find that thoughts, in turn, are vibrations of *consciousness*—that consciousness is, in fact, the underlying reality of *everything*. In fact, it will be truer to say that consciousness *is* everything, not merely *underlying* everything. Vibrations of consciousness have produced every-thing in existence. There *is* no other reality.

"This world *is conscious*. We might wonder, Is it *self*-conscious? Does it have feelings? Certainly, in the rocks, consciousness is dormant. (I wouldn't think of sitting down to a game of checkers with a rock!) But somehow there *is* a kind of self-consciousness in everything. There is also feeling, even in the worms—in the very atoms.

"Those pulsations you've heard in the tunnel are vibrations of feeling. On the outside of the tunnel, above and around its sides, my father and I placed innumerable layers of crystals. The sunlight, passing through those crystals, energizes them. That's why we built our laboratory against a cliff, to catch the sunlight also reflected off the rocks. The crystals hum in sympathy with the energy-vibrations of the earth. That vibratory movement, expressed as a hum, is *inwardly* self-canceling. It eliminates size, and therefore also space. Without space there is no movement, and then time also ceases to exist. And (as you saw) after passing through the tunnel one emerges from time into timelessness." Hansel looked at the boys meaningly.

"Have you *any* idea what he's talking about," Bobby asked his older brother.

"None!" Donny exclaimed.

"But it's so *simple*!" protested Hansel. "Motion in space is what creates the illusion of time. Without space, there would be no motion, and, therefore, no time!"

"I'm sure you know best," said Bobby conciliatingly.

"Can we change the subject?" Donny asked a little desperately. "What interests *me* is those men we saw yesterday, in Romania and later in Switzerland. Vlad, first, and his soldiers: The prisoners were frightened almost to death, but the other men stood about, laughing—what about them? Even in their laughter they didn't really seem *happy*. The same was obviously true of Gessler and *his* men. What I think is that, although those people may have enjoyed power, they didn't enjoy *themselves*."

"That is very true," Hansel said. "People who perform wrong actions suffer inwardly in some way. It's one of the perceptions one gains from time travel: one quickly sees that what makes an act or an attitude wrong is that it simply doesn't work— *especially* not for the person himself. And you get to see what *does* work, and also what works even better. The more you *help* others, for instance, the happier you become, yourself! You can learn this lesson better when the scenes before you are remote from your own personal realities, for then you can see them more objectively."

Donny pondered this point, then said, "Most people, probably, would say that the reason Vlad suffered—if he did suffer—was that he knew everybody hated him. But with someone as insensitive as he, I think he must have gloried in the fact."

Hansel said, "Really, what must have got to him, in the end, was that he ended up hating himself! His self-hatred became layered over with self-justification, and with hatred and contempt for everyone else. People's main problem is that they are centered too much in themselves. They know instinctively that they are part of a consciousness which exists everywhere! So they try to emphasize their little selves by layering them over with self-definitions. These increase in number until they become intolerable; the sheer weight of them can press a person almost to the ground. It's the burden itself they hate, not themselves! But they don't know how to distinguish between themselves and that burden, so they keep on adding more and more self-definitions to their already-existing, increasingly intolerable burden.

"What Vlad carried about with him was his own indifference to people's suffering. What he found overwhelmingly heavy was the wall he was building around himself—determined as he was to exclude everyone from his sympathies."

Donny said, "What could be more unrealistic than to try to exclude other people's realities from one's own?"

"That wasn't how Vlad saw it," Hansel replied. "He told himself he wanted to be *realistic*. Therefore he hardened his heart's feelings. The hard shell he built around his heart became, for him, the burden which filled him with anger against everyone, because he felt it was other people who had forced him to create that shell. Poor Vlad had tied himself into mental and emotional knots! He suffered more deeply than any of those he was causing pain. His problem was that, by killing his own feelings, he also killed his own potential for happiness!"

Bobby piped up, "He should have seen that he was no better than anyone else!"

"The way to do that," said Donny thoughtfully, "would have been to see that he was no *different* from them—or from anybody else."

Hansel remarked, "And how could he do that, when his life was devoted to *emphasizing* the differences—as he imagined them to be? All people have basically the same needs: food and rest, for example, and happiness. Vlad's heart-feelings were as clogged as a stuffed stomach by indigestion of feelings! He fed those feelings on leaden selfhood, even as some people feed their stomachs with heavy food."

"Such a person," mused Donny, "could never produce anything worthwhile in this world. Everything he did would bring misery—to others, but most of all to himself!"

"That makes me think again of Egypt," said Bobby. "How could any nation that endorsed slavery have built such a noble structure as the Great Pyramid?"

"You are right in calling it a noble structure," Hansel said. "Its very purpose *was* noble. It was built to *help* people. Certainly it wasn't built as a monument to power. Anyone who thinks that great monument could serve such a low purpose knows almost nothing about human nature. Slave power? Apart from the fact that slaves would have had to bring those huge rocks up very long ramps, which, again, would have had to be changed in height constantly, and stretched much too far to be practicable— apart from all that, I say, slavery just wasn't the way people were dreaming in those days. What they did, in fact, was rely on the kind of vibrations my father and I built into our time tunnel."

"You mean," Donny said, "you built the tunnel so that it would *receive* those vibrations?"

"Right!" said Hansel. "The vibrations were there already. The whole universe is a manifestation of vibration. Vibrations both produce and *are produced* by *sound*. Different sound vibrations are associated with different levels of vibration. Energy, in order to produce matter, first vibrated a sound rather like that which is made by wind in the trees, or like an ocean roar: a soothing, *rushing* sound.

"Energy then vibrated more grossly, producing gasses. This vibrational sound was like a deep gong, or like large temple bells ringing out over the countryside.

"Energy vibrating still more grossly produced the fiery gasses that manifest the stars. Its sound was subtle, like that of a plucked string instrument.

"Energy vibrating still more grossly produced liquids such as molten metals, and also water. That vibration created a fluid sound like that produced by a flute, or by flowing water.

"And energy, finally, vibrating most grossly of all produced solid matter, which made a low humming sound—like what you boys heard in the time tunnel. That sound gradually dissolved you back from time into timelessness."

"So that's what we heard?" cried Bobby. "It was the vibrations of the earth itself?"

"The people who created the pyramid lived in an age much higher than our own," said Hansel. "They knew how to manipulate sounds, and possessed innumerable instruments— big drums for the low hum of solid earth; flutes for liquid matter; harps for fiery matter; deep gongs for gaseous matter; and a rushing sound produced by an instrument that is unknown today.

"In addition, many priests and priestesses loudly chanted certain sacred sounds. All of these sounds together *lifted* the huge rocks into place, and inserted them between the other stones in a way that researchers have long marveled over. For in fact those stones could not have been placed so precisely except *from above*. And no one could possibly have placed them *downward* without the use of huge cranes, which would have been clumsy and quite incapable of creating the perfect fit those large blocks of stone received."

"Oh, *my!*" exclaimed Donny. "This is *thrilling!* To think that mankind can ever accomplish such feats! Why don't we go there and see for ourselves?"

They scrolled up their time-light spheres, accordingly, and found themselves suddenly on a wide, sandy plateau. They remained in their spheres, invisible and inaudible from the outside, but found it easy to communicate with one another.

Before them, they saw layers upon layers of massive stone blocks, the structure rising to ever-narrower proportions.

"It does seem to me that the Great Pyramid could not have been built by slave labor," said Donny. "Mother said it was built by the pharaoh Khufu, as his tomb."

"The pyramid never served any such purpose!" Hansel cried indignantly. "Khufu added his name, as did other pharaohs of his era to ancient monuments, with a view to claiming for themselves some of the glories of the past. The fantasy of slave labor was created by very ordinary men, incapable of imagining any high purpose. Nothing has ever been found in that so-called tomb, however: no gold, no treasures, and—the clincher—no human body. It has always been empty. The function of the perfectly-formed so-called sarcophagus, which was found in the so-called burial chamber, was entirely different. Curiously, no lid for it has ever been discovered. More recent scholars have supposed that the Great Pyramid was built for initiation purposes."

Bobby quite naturally asked, "What's inchen?"

Hansel explained, "Initiation is a special ceremony where priests were taught things that they alone were supposed to know. For example, during those rites they may have learned how to chant certain prayers in such a way as to generate power."

"Like, 'Hail Mary, full of grace . . .'?" asked Bobby.

"Well, something like that," conceded Hansel. "Anyway, that's what certain scholars have guessed was its purpose. Others have had less interesting theories. At least the supporters of the 'initiation' theory have understood that the Great Pyramid had a higher purpose than merely to serve as a glorified tomb!"

"But why did they build such a huge structure, anyway," Donny asked, "if it was only to hold a little casket for private initiations?"

"The so-called 'tomb,'" said Hansel, "was meant for something *much* greater. And it wasn't built for people who wanted to *receive* anything, whether burial or secret initiation. It was built so that spiritually developed priests and priestesses might *give out* blessings from there to the whole world.

"One interesting fact about Egypt," Hansel concluded, "is that it started, as a civilization, at its height. There is no indication of an earlier rise from obscurity. It has been theorized that Egypt was a colony of Atlantis, which, if you like, we may visit later."

"Do you mean," Donny asked, "that all of Egypt's known history has been *downhill?*"

"That's what the evidence shows," Hansel answered. "Egypt also was situated more or less—as those scholars have pointed out—at the center of the land mass of the earth. The Great Pyramid, they claim, stands at the *very* center."

The three of them watched the construction of the pyramid rising quickly, as they swept forward over the years it took for that monument to be finished. Suddenly they saw before them—not a great pile of rocks, but a smooth, gleaming white limestone structure, reflecting a shining light for many miles over the flat desert.

"Outside one of the gates into the city of Rome," Hansel told them, "there stands a much smaller pyramid. It doesn't look like the Great Pyramid today, because it is still covered by smooth, white limestone. That was what the Great Pyramid looked like at first. Centuries later, when modern Cairo was built, people took the surface stone from the pyramid to construct their homes. Half of Cairo was built, I've heard, with stones from the Great Pyramid. Long ago, it wasn't the massive pile of blocks people see today. Instead, the pyramid stood gleaming like a giant gemstone in the desert.

"As people will discover in time," Hansel continued, "the pyramid shape creates a special energy. Inside it, people's consciousness is heightened."

Donny interrupted at this point to say, "What do you mean by heightened?"

Hansel smiled again. "What I mean is that people became more intensely *aware* of everything. It's like (only much more so) when you wake up from sleep in the morning. Instead of lying there thinking lightly about things (as people often do in the morning), a person in heightened consciousness is completely *absorbed* in a greater wakefulness. He isn't thinking at all. You *know*, when you are in that state, that you are *completely— thrillingly* alive!"

"Oh, I think I know what you mean!" cried Donny. "When I was much younger, I used to see lights in bed at night when I closed my eyes. I saw beautiful scenes also. Well," he went on to admit, "there were other nights when I was too scared to put a hand out beyond the edge of my bed for fear of that panther I knew was hiding underneath it, waiting to grab me!"

Hansel smiled, then commented, "Well, there's a 'panther' of subconscious fears lurking in most people's minds. The Great Pyramid was meant to help raise people's consciousness above those fears. And the pyramid housed another chamber, too— lower in that great structure. In the upper chamber, priests of great spiritual power would lie in the casket and send power out from the pyramid to all the world. Men's energy is different from women's. For proper balance, there needed to be also priestesses, sending out a more all-embracing energy. The two together, priests and priestesses, working from their respective chambers within the energy-generating pyramid, radiated great power to all the world, and great protection for Egypt itself."

"What did that power do," Bobby asked.

"It brought kindness to the world, and peace, and happiness. It was a completely *good* power," Hansel answered. "Shall we wait and see?"

Time suddenly slipped forward into the future, like a recorded tape fast-forwarding—only in this case what rushed by were not sounds, but scenes.

Time suddenly stopped. A priest and a priestess entered the Great Pyramid. Our three friends followed the priest in their time-light spheres. They saw him lie down in the open casket.

"As I mentioned, they've never found a lid for that casket," said Hansel. "And the casket itself, amazingly, was carved from a single block of stone! I know of no modern tools that could have accomplished that feat so perfectly."

The priest lay down inside the casket, and, smiling blissfully, closed his eyes—and stopped breathing altogether!

"How did he do *that*?" Bobby asked.

"He entered a heightened state of consciousness," explained Hansel.

The three could actually *feel* peace flow over them like a shower of light. They sat in silence for a time, basking in that peace, and feeling cleansed by it.

"Centuries later," Hansel said, "the world began to lose its high spiritual consciousness. The natives of Egypt began then to think only of manipulating shapes and sounds to gain power for themselves. Gradually they fell into what at first was ordinary magic, but later took on the form of black magic. People tried to hurt one another with their power. Egypt itself, then, and the whole African continent, fell into a darkness of superstition, seething with the lust for destruction.

"Soon now, in your present time, Africa will begin again to rise and resume its rightful place among the prosperous (because righteous) nations."

"Oh, Hansel!" cried Donny. "You're opening up such a view of history! It could stagger all humanity!"

"Yes," Hansel commented, "but maybe it is time for people to *be* staggered! Ignorance is too prevalent today, for that is the way people are still dreaming. Because human consciousness is materialistic, people can't imagine a reality higher than that of matter. But in fact this earth is part of a cosmic environment. It passes through fluctuating influences. The intensity of human awareness rises and falls, as I said, like waves. There have been higher civilizations than ours in the past, and also lower ones. We are now on a rising wave of awareness. The future will see sweeping changes for the better. Mankind will even travel to distant planets—perhaps to distant galaxies, since time and space, both, are cosmic delusions!"

"Wow!" cried Bobby. "And what do you suppose will happen *then*?"

"The sky, they say, is the limit! Shall we try going to the future—maybe tomorrow?"

Bobby said. "Oh, but I think I'd like first to go to Atlantis—since you mentioned it!"

"*Atlantis!*" cried Donny. "I know nothing about it. But people say they were highly advanced then. Do let's go there first!"

"Very well, then," Hansel concluded. "Tomorrow: Atlantis!"

They returned in their time-light spheres to their starting point, re-entered the tunnel, had a leisurely swim in the brook—all these things that same day! And then: supper, and bed.

CHAPTER 7

Atlantis!

HEY WERE SEATED THE FOLLOWING DAY ON the sward. (A "sward," dear readers, is a grassy lawn. I thought the "Donnys" among you might like to learn this word.) In fact, Hansel very soon used it himself.

"Let's sit here on the sward," he said.

"'Sward!' muttered Donny. "It sounds like 'sword,' but instead of cutting anything, it gets cut! *Sward.*"

"What was Atlantis like?" inquired Bobby, eager with anticipation. The boys had been talking about it in hush-hush voices together ever since yesterday's outing—or was it yesterday's *inning*!

"I once asked Daddy about it," said Donny, "and he answered, 'It can't have existed.' He went on to talk about 'content drift,' or something." (Of course the term Donny was trying to remember was "continental drift.")

"Well, here's something to think about," said Hansel: "Atlantis was situated (this seems obvious) in the Atlantic Ocean. The nearest landmass westward probably was Mexico. Consider, then, the names of many cities in Mexico today: Acatlán; Mazatlán; Zacatlán; and names without the first or the second 'a,' but with that strange 'tlán' sound: Ixtlán; Ocotlán; Tepoztlán; Tezuitlán. Often you can find clues to the past in the sounds of language itself. I don't believe that 'tlán' sound can be found anywhere else on earth. Certainly it must be very uncommon. And, as part of the same puzzle, what about the Atlantic Ocean itself? I know of no connection between that name and any ancient language. Where did it come from?"

"Gee," said Donny thoughtfully, "that *is* a good argument!"

"And anyway, I've been there!" said Hansel, clinching the matter. "Atlantis *existed* all right! Moreover, I think there has been too much written about it for it *not* to have existed. It's as if there were a sort of race memory of human beings having once actually lived there. More and more, in our immediate future, people will be born with an instinctive—perhaps even Atlantean—knowledge of the sciences.

"Atlantis was a very high civilization," Hansel continued. "On it, at its center, there was a huge crystal. That crystal provided energy for the whole island."

"You say the Atlanteans were a scientific people?" Donny asked.

"Too much so!" said Hansel. "We talked of *sward* a moment ago. They didn't have much grass there. Everything was man-made and artificial. They believed in *conquering* Nature, not in working *with* her."

"Why do you say *her*?" Bobby asked. "Why not *it*?"

"Well, isn't Nature like a mother? I've said that everything manifests consciousness. Doesn't Nature as a whole almost seem conscious? She *gives* life: she doesn't just produce it, as if out of a drawer. Things grow gradually from seeds into plants. Everything grows out from its own center. Man, instead, carves his statues from the outside, but Nature *grows* living forms from the inside—from their center. Nature, surely, *is* just like a great mother."

"But then Nature wasn't treated with proper respect by the Atlanteans?" asked Donny.

"I'm afraid not," Hansel answered. "They wanted, as I said, to conquer her. I told you grass didn't grow there. Of course they had *some* grass, and *some* trees. But meadows? forests? I've never seen any. What I meant to say was that the Atlanteans didn't *appreciate* Nature. They didn't *love* her. A beautiful sunset set the Atlanteans to thinking how the sunlight might be used to generate more power, or how those colors might be used to filter electricity in new ways. A tree would be seen only in terms of the elements that might be extracted from it for chemical or medicinal uses. The Atlanteans might be described as super-scientists, for they tried to suppress all feeling in the name of cold reason."

"What a *dry* outlook!" cried Bobby.

"Yes," Hansel commented. "People who try to exclude their hearts' feelings become little more than machines—robots! things to be *used*. And the people of Atlantis began to see human beings in that light also: as instruments to be merely *used*."

"That," Bobby said, "would take all the fun out of living!"

"Well, there you have the Atlanteans! They decided they didn't want fun: they wanted *power*. Of course, what they really wanted—what everybody really wants—was *happiness*; no one can ever help wanting that. But the Atlanteans tried to find happiness through power. Unfortunately for them, lacking the ability to have fun, it wasn't even faintly possible for them to find happiness!"

"So why did they want power?" asked Bobby.

"They wanted it because they thought it would make them bigger. But bigness isn't....Well, why don't we just travel back there in time and see for ourselves?"

They enclosed themselves in their time-light spheres, and Hansel (who knew where to go) willed the three of them back thousands of years ago, to ancient Atlantis.

On arrival they found themselves in a gleamingly white city—super clean, super neat in construction, super efficient, super—well, super everything! High buildings towered around them. People rode about in neat, small metal "sheaths" of cars, easily avoiding contact with one another. If one car happened to touch another, the surfaces of both cars adjusted instantly, bending inward softly to avoid any damaging clash.

One thing the boys noted instantly was a virtual absence of noise. Motors were silent. Cars didn't actually touch the ground: They floated an inch or two above it. No car horns sounded. A public transport passed by silently, carrying many passengers, but (again) floated lightly just above the ground. The buses—I suppose we'll still have to call them that—looked comfortable, welcoming, and spacious enough inside not to be crowded, but though in some ways they resembled our buses, they emitted no fumes. And they, too, moved silently.

There seemed to be no need for traffic lights, for although the north-south flow occurred at ground level, the east-west flow was on some sort of translucent street one floor above them.

Traffic never seemed to clog or get jammed, but flowed smoothly and silently. When a car stopped, whether to let out passengers or simply to park, it did so in the right lane of whatever direction it was flowing, then instantly rose three storeys to a translucent sidewalk, where everyone in it got out, and the car moved on to a large building, where it was housed. Some sort of invisible radio force seemed to take over from the moment the driver and any passengers descended.

On the streets there were no sidewalks. The sidewalks were indoors, two storeys up, and passed over the cross streets. Much was made possible by the fact that the construction material, though in appearance it resembled white marble, was translucent. The streets below were not plunged in deep shadow, and those above didn't create confusing shadows beneath them. The streets, where they crossed one another, created gaps between the lines of buildings, and produced the same city blocks we ourselves know. But instead of shops at the ground level, beautiful murals were displayed: not paintings, but fascinating, ever-changing patterns of colored light. All this made passing though the city an exhilarating and—for anyone accustomed to the crowds, smells, noise, and confusion of modern cities—an altogether beautiful experience.

Our three friends (Hansel had decided to give them this experience) scrolled down their time-light spheres on the lowest level, where—unfortunately for them!—there was no sidewalk. Instantly they discovered the inconvenience of walking on that level, as the traffic had to make a small detour around them. Our three, however, walked side by side a little distance down the street.

"What did you say about people's attitude here?" Bobby asked, dodging right as a car brushed very close to him.

"Not down here!" shouted a man angrily, as he emerged hastily from a doorway. He wore an official-looking uniform, and seemed quite indignant. "What are you doing down here in the traffic flow? Get upstairs where you belong!"

"Upstairs?" asked Bobby. "*Where* upstairs?"

"Oh, for Crystal's sake! Step on that flat square over there. It will take you up. Don't you have any *sense*?"

"Sorry, Sir, we're from out of town," Donny said. They stepped onto the flat square. Suddenly a wall of light formed around them, and they found themselves transported two storeys up to a translucent sidewalk. Looking down, they saw the roofs of cars passing beneath them. These shone with millions of tiny points of light. Beside them they saw a beautiful shop window displaying styles of clothing which they'd never seen or even ever imagined before. Fascinated, they entered an open doorway. Evidently, there was no need for doors to protect the air inside from that which was outside. The atmosphere of both was clean, and—as the boys commented in whispers to each other—there was evidently no need to exclude the nonexistent noise.

Hansel, overhearing them, added, "There's a huge, transparent dome over the whole city. It keeps the air inside at just the right temperature, and eliminates flies and other insects. So you see— outer doors are not necessary here!"

They went inside. Just then, a lady passing them in the same direction cried out, "Great Crystal! What are you three doing dressed like *that*!" She was wearing something that looked almost liquid; it flowed gracefully around her, softening her form.

"These clothes are all we've got!" cried Bobby.

"Oh, let me take you to a section here where they sell men's and boys' clothing."

"But we've no money with which to pay for it!"

"Oh, don't be silly!" the woman scoffed kindly. "Just sign your names. They'll go instantly into the credit pool. All you need do is give them your address."

"Well," Donny started to explain, "we don't really have an address."

"No address!" the woman exclaimed. "Where do you live— out on some sort of *farm*, or something?"

"Well," said Donny hesitantly, "you might call it that. It's more like a farm than anything I see around here."

"Great Crystal! I didn't know anything like that still existed in this country. We grow our food on rooftops, in trays containing treated liquid." She made a slightly wry face. "The food's good enough, I guess, though I admit I liked it better when it grew in the ground. Still, we've gone beyond all that now! So anyway, just look around and see if there's anything you like. I'll just leave you here," she concluded. "I have errands to run."

Looking around, the boys saw trays that contained shorts for boys their own age, and fingered the clothing. The fabric seemed almost liquid to the touch, folding softly around their hands while still maintaining its own integrity.

"Wow! what *colors*!" they exclaimed in unison. Donny added, "So vivid! so—*inviting*!"

Bobby exclaimed, "I especially like this bright, bright red material. It's so cheerful, it makes me want to smile."

A saleslady came over to them with a grim expression. "Yes," she said, "that color sells well. And it'll make people sit up and *listen* to you."

"But I don't *want* people to 'sit up and listen!' It's enough if they don't play deaf and dumb when I speak."

"A wimp, eh? Well then, for you, green would be better."

"But I *like* this red!" objected Bobby.

"Then get used to having people sit up and listen, or even cringe before you!" the saleslady answered dismissively.

"Oh, I don't like what you're saying! Just give me the red. I'll see to it that nobody cringes."

"They won't cringe if you order them not to," said the woman.

"Creepy!" muttered Bobby under his breath to Donny.

"What I like," Donny said, going to another counter, "is this scrumptious blue! Just look at it, Bobby! Remember that sea voyage we took two years ago, when we stopped in Italy and went into the Blue Grotto on the island of Capri? That deep, rich, liquid blue! Oh, I *like* this! Where's the changing room?" he asked the lady.

"There's no need for one," she told him a little brusquely. "Where are you folks *from*, anyway? Just press the button by this counter. An envelope of light will surround you and block anyone else's gaze. When you're finished, press the button again."

Donny did as she'd told him. Suddenly, from the outside, he became invisibly enclosed in a tall, narrow column of light. When he emerged in his new shorts, he commented, "I could see you, Bobby! Could you *really* not see me?"

"Not at all," said Bobby. "All I saw was that column of light all the way to the ceiling."

"Now, let's get some shirts to match," said Donny. They went over to a new counter, where they found the same liquid-seeming material, firm enough to cohere, but flowing and not so easy to feel. It was in the same brilliant colors. There seemed, however, to be no stitches, and the sleeves and shoulders had a continuous flow from the trunk to the arms, without distinct shoulders.

"I don't know that I like this," Donny said. "I like to know where my shoulders are."

"Let's try one on," said Bobby.

"Where are the buttons?" Donny cried, holding a shirt up for inspection.

Just then another saleslady came over. All efficiency, she asked, "May I help you boys?"

"Yes," said Donny. "Where are the buttons?"

"The—*what?*" asked the lady, giving them a blank look.

"Buttons—those round things for getting into a shirt and holding it on you. Don't tell me you don't know what *buttons* are!"

"No," said the saleslady brusquely. "I really don't know what you're talking about. To get into this shirt, just hold it against your back and pull it around you."

"Oh my gosh!" cried Bobby, doing so with a bright red shirt he'd found. "It works! *How* does it work?"

"Well," said Donny, donning a beautiful blue shirt he'd selected, "it seems to be kind of like water, but you can hold it. It's sort of like being in our shower back in Teleajen, and letting the spray come around our bodies from behind. But if I can bring it forward so easily, wouldn't the lightest touch pull it back again?"

"No," said the saleslady, puzzled at their ignorance. "Once it fits your body, it stays there until you dry it off with a towel."

"Well then," asked Bobby, "how do you put it back on again?"

"You just wring the towel out into a basin, silly! Then pick the shirt up and hang it in your closet. When you want to put it on again, just put it on your back like before and pull it around you. Simple, isn't it?" She looked with raised eyebrows at another saleslady, who had been standing there observing this quaint manifestation of country bumpkinism.

Just then Hansel approached them from the men's section. He, too, had been exploring. They saw him dressed in a beautiful, flowing cape of some kind, colored a sumptuous yellow.

"How do you like it?" he asked with a smile, twirling around so they could see the cape flow out around him. Underneath it, he wore long trousers and a shirt, both garments made of a material similar to what the boys were wearing.

"We'd better keep our old clothes with us in a bag," said Hansel, "for when we go back to timelessness. The zone we're in now is only dream-time."

"Dream-time!" exclaimed one of the salesladies. She had been standing close enough to hear him. In fact, our three friends had begun to create quite a stir among the salespeople. "Say, where do you folks come from, anyway. This is no dream! It's perfectly real. See," she said, and, reaching out, she gave Bobby a pinch on the arm. "I can touch you. And," she cried triumphantly as Bobby winced, "you can *feel* it!"

"Let's not go into all that!" was Hansel's hasty remark. "Why don't we just get on with our purchases? The lady who brought us here said we could pay for all this from the credit pool. What did she mean?"

"You're telling me you don't even know what the *credit pool* is!?" cried the saleslady unbelievingly.

"Is it something liquid, like these clothes?" asked Bobby. Donny gave him a slight shove as a hint to be more careful with his questions. "Is it something we can dive into," Bobby persisted. "Will we get wet all over?"

"A credit pool," said the saleslady with a long-suffering glance at her companions, "is something everybody *belongs* to. It's a sort of society."

"But if they don't get wet," Hansel commented dryly, "they may get splashed in another way that they don't like at all!"

"Here, just sign your names on this line!" said the lady impatiently.

At that moment the lady they'd first met on coming into the store entered this clothing section, and approached them.

"Is everything all right?" she asked with a kindly smile. Seeing the boys' puzzlement, she asked, "What's the trouble?"

"These folks claim to know nothing about the credit pool!" said the saleslady. "And I'm wondering: Are they from some other planet?"

"That's all right," their first friend assured her. "I'll take care of it." She showed the saleslady a bracelet on her wrist, from which the lady wrote down something. While she was writing, their friend said to them, "By the way, my name is Mrs. Besintlan. May I know your names?"

Donny told her, then whispered, "I'm so glad we've met you! All the people here act as if they'd be happy if we actually *were* from some place like Venus, and went back there!"

Mrs. Besintlan gave them a motherly smile, then said, "Well, that's taken care of. I've finished my errands. Since you folks are strangers. . . ." (The actual word, or concept, she conveyed was "barbarians," but her expression told them she didn't mean it insultingly.) "Let me take you to a shop above here. The food section is below on the bottom two floors. Trucks come in there, bringing produce to that section from lower entrances. But upstairs the shops are more interesting."

She led them up by standing first on another rising plate in the hallway outside, around which a wall of light rose instantly, protectively. They emerged onto another hallway teeming with people, all of them comfortably dressed in liquid-seeming clothes, and all hurrying to their own destinations.

"By the way," said Donny, "what was that light we saw on the roofs of cars in the street below?"

"Those were millions of tiny crystals," Mrs. Besintlan answered. "The crystals absorb sunlight—and even ordinary daylight on a cloudy day—converting it to the power which enables the cars to move silently."

"My goodness!" Bobby exclaimed. "Just think what *that*

would do for the smelly streets of Bucharest!"

They came to a store containing what might be called a general assortment of appliances.

"I think this store will please you," said their companion, leading them inside. Here they came upon a clothes-washer that used only light. A dishwasher, in another section, sprayed a kind of liquid light onto slightly flexible dishes, when these were placed inside it. It then gave them what seemed like a splash of light, and rolled out the dishes, gleamingly clean, separating and stacking them neatly. Each dish got placed among others of its kind: bowls with bowls; large plates with large plates; saucers with saucers, etc.

In another section they found a stove which, instead of applying heat outwardly to the food it cooked, heated the food from within. I guess nowadays we'd compare it to a microwave oven, but this device looked very different.

There was a mixing bowl which mixed food not with blades, but with sound vibrations that emitted a tone inaudible to the human ear.

In another section of the shop they found gadgets that shaved or cut hair with sound; cleaned teeth with light; another gadget that scratched your back without touching it, using only sound.

Mrs. Besintlan led them into a toy section. Here they found little discs that could be stood upon, with rods that could be gripped firmly. This "air scooter," as Bobby promptly dubbed it, lifted its rider off the ground by some sort of magnetic force, then sailed him across the floor. Bobby stood on one such scooter, but twisted the handle too vigorously: In an instant he was shooting across the room, and crashed into a wall. The wall gave, however—as if politely!—not hurting him at all.

"Oh!" cried Donny, "and look at this gadget over here." It

was a tower of light, radiating what might almost be termed "*delicious*" colors! Donny stepped inside it; his voice could be heard through the light, but, again, he was invisible from outside it. "Oh!" he cried. "How *wonderful*! How *exciting*! How *beautiful*!" Emerging from the tower, his eyes were shining. "Everything inside," he reported in amazement, "was like a brilliant shower of colored lights!"

"How thrilling!" cried Bobby, and entered the tower, experiencing the lights also.

Mrs. Besintlan then said, "Let me show you also another group of toys. These may be for children a bit younger than you, Bobby, but they're fun. They're called Dancing Bears."

She led them to a tray on which lay an assortment of teddy bears. Picking up one of them, they saw that its eyes displayed a variety of changing expressions depending on how many times one squeezed the bear from the side. One expression was proud; another timid; still another, amused. All the teddy bears were comically fat, and, with their short, stubby legs, ungainly. Each bear bore a label on its lower back.

Mrs. Besintlan said, "This bear is labeled, 'Ballet.' Now, let me set it on this surface over here." She set it on a flat tray, one foot square, on the same counter. "Now, watch!"

She clapped her hands once. Suddenly the bear rose on its hind legs and began to perform an absurd parody of classical ballet movements and positions. All the while, a recording of ballet music, played with high fidelity by a full, unseen orchestra, issued from the bear's belly.

The two boys, and also Hansel, laughed delightedly, then clapped their hands loudly in applause. Immediately the "bear" stopped dancing, bowed in a rich parody of solemnity, and sat down again.

Mrs. Besintlan said, "You must clap differently to keep the bear moving. More than one quick clap stops its dancing altogether. One clap starts it off. If you want to show enthusiasm, clap more slowly. The bear will then continue dancing."

"Oh, what fun!" cried Donny. "Is there another dance you can show us?"

Mrs. Besintlan answered, "Well, would you like to see a flamenco dance?"

"What's that?" Donny asked.

"It's something from the future," she said casually. "Let me show you." She returned the teddy bear to the tray, and picked up another one labeled, "Flamenco." This time, once she'd set the bear on the tray and it began dancing, the music that emerged was of an energetically played guitar. The bear then proceeded proudly to demonstrate, extremely ludicrously, a number of supposedly elegant, but in fact highly *in*elegant flamenco movements.

They all laughed uproariously.

Mrs. Besintlan then set the bear back on its tray.

"Isn't that enough excitement for one morning?" she asked. "Would you like to come to my home for lunch?"

"Oh, would we *ever*!" cried Bobby. As the others began to leave, however, he sneaked back and accosted a salesclerk, a rather dour looking, seamy-faced man, and whispered. "Could I buy that air scooter?"

"That *what*? Oh, I see," said the man. "Of course! You could pay for it out of the credit pool. All you need to do is sign here." He held out a paper pad, on which Bobby signed his name.

"How can I carry it?" Bobby asked.

"Oh, I know Mrs. Besintlan," the clerk assured him. "I will just have it sent to her home."

"Oh," Bobby cried, "thanks a *zillion*!"

"Yes, Sir," said the man matter-of-factly. From his words, one would have thought he was addressing a grown-up instead of a little child of seven—well, seven and a half! Bobby straightened his shoulders a little self-importantly, then rushed off to find the others. He caught them just as they reached the entrance to the store. Mrs. Besintlan took a sort of wand out of her handbag, and uttered a brief command into it. Her car slid up to the entrance just as the four of them emerged from the entrance. They got in, descended one storey, and smoothly entered the traffic flow.

Mrs. Besintlan's "home" was very different from anything they'd seen before. For one thing, it was only an apartment, not a separate building out in the country. But for another, its translucent outer walls shone softly with ever-changing pastel colors of light.

The furniture in the room was adequate, but not startlingly so, except for the fact that, although no seat was cushioned, when the boys sat down they found the seats yielding comfortably to the pressure of their bodies, adjusting to them without absorbing them.

Most of one large, opaque wall at the back of the living room contained a huge television screen. This bit wasn't homelike or beautiful at all. On the screen they beheld a grim-faced man staring fiercely out into the room, and seeming from the way his mouth worked to be ranting about something. They couldn't make out the words, however, as the volume was very low.

"I'm afraid I can't turn off that picture," their hostess told them apologetically. "In any case I wouldn't be allowed to do so. But at least I can turn down the volume!" She didn't seem to care much for the "entertainment" being offered.

Bobby went over to a system of controls. Curious to hear what was being said, he twirled a knob that increased the volume slightly. Suddenly there surged into the room a loud diatribe.

"Citizens," thundered the speaker, "I, Gorbatlani, your benign and ever-protective dictator, plead with you for *your own good* to heed my words! Those who—disloyal to our glorious nation—fail to do so will be shipped off to the western colonies! Atlanteans *shall* stand firmly united behind the will of the people! *I* am your power, your strength, and your glory! Atlanteans: Stand up firm before your nefarious enemies!

"I am here this evening to discuss a shocking incident that occurred this morning. There have been murmurs—by Crystal's grace, very few!—prejudicial to the welfare of the citizens of Atlantis! Protests against official policies, and against the laws which we, your ever-benign rulers, have enacted for your well-being! Yes, it happens inevitably, even in our glorious country, that persons occasionally get born who are sick—not only mentally, but still worse: politically!

"This morning a demonstration occurred in a certain square of our capital—I won't mention which square—during which an attempt was made to arouse people against our rule. Loyal proclamation-enforcers were there, of course." The man smirked. "The agitators will soon be languishing in a distant colony! But I am here today to tell you: I—yes, I, Gorbatlani the Great— such dissonance to disturb the peace of our society. I've been empowered by our Great Crystal to bring Atlantis to its present state of shining perfection! For Atlantis"—his expression at this point melted into teary sentimentality, "is like a beautiful fugue! Yes," he repeated, shedding "crocodile" tears, "a fugue of order and discipline, in which *every note* keeps its proper place, beats its correct time, and produces its predestined harmonies. Oh, I tell you this: Troublemakers will have their reward! But I plead with every loyal citizen to report *anyone* who even whispers against our great and noble land. Disloyalty, *even of thought,* is treachery, punishable by a fate even worse than execution: exile into outer darkness!

"Think what that will mean:"—his expression now assumed a look of drenching pity—"no beautiful, translucent buildings; no wonderful, artificially produced air; no chemically enhanced foods; no comfortable, *beautiful,* body-wrapping clothes! Oh, what a *wonderful* life we lead here, my fellow Atlanteans! Let us thank our Great Crystal for what we have been given!"

He kneeled, and a large choir in the background sang with him enthusiastically:

Crys-tal, so great and wise,

Shine on our paradise!

   Bless a-all who-o worship Thee.

Glo-o-ry: A-rise!

Mrs. Besintlan came over to Bobby and, with a light chuckle, turned the volume as nearly off as it would go.

"If I kept it turned high enough to listen to," she said, "I'd be overwhelmed by that frightful garbage all day long! When our 'glorious dictator' isn't speaking, some other official is up there spouting the same dreadful message."

"I'm shocked!" cried Donny. "At first, everything seemed to me so ideal!"

"The sweetness of honey attracts flies!" Hansel pointed out.

"But it wasn't sweetness that produced the 'perfection' you've encountered here!" commented Mrs. Besintlan. "It was control. They're completely obsessed here with power and control—control over *everything* and *everyone*! Wherever we turn, we find 'them' there, breathing down our backs. They don't work *with*

Nature; they work *against* her, trying to bend her to their will. Yes, they do see her as a mother, but to them she's someone to be scolded, bullied, and wheedled into giving them what they want—as if she had no will to give anything freely of her own abundance!"

Hansel said, "You're showing me a side I hadn't understood so clearly before. But this does seem to be a completely unbalanced society. Men are trying to dominate everything—not only Nature, but the rest of mankind."

"Yes," said their hostess, "*men!*" She emphasized that word with bitter irony. "Woman, certainly, is suppressed here."

"I see no hope," said Hansel, "for any society that emphasizes the merits of one sex alone. But," he added sadly, "Atlantis is going to be destroyed—and fairly soon now, I think."

"What do you mean?" asked Mrs. Besintlan.

"Mother Earth," Hansel explained, "won't stand for such abuse much longer." The boys looked apprehensively from one adult to the other.

"What's this all about?" asked Donny.

Just then there came a loud pounding on the front door. "Open up!" came a stern command from outside.

Mrs. Besintlan fearfully opened the front door. Six officers of the law stepped inside. "Bobby Walters?" one of them demanded in stentorian tones.

"That's me," said Bobby, his voice quaking.

"Mr. Walters," shouted the official, "You've charged to the credit pool this package we've brought with us. Investigation has revealed that you do not belong to our glorious credit pool. Further investigation has revealed that you are not even inscribed as a citizen of our glorious nation. You are guilty of two crimes against the laws of our noble land." At this, all six men saluted gravely, raising their right hands and shouting, "Hail Gorbatlani!"

"But I didn't know I was doing anything wrong," cried Bobby. "Please take that scooter back. I no longer want it."

"Ignorance of the law is a further crime against the fatherland," shouted the spokesman. "You will be transported to the colonies. In consideration of your age, the normally obligatory lashes will be eliminated!"

"I'll come with him!" Donny cried staunchly.

"And so will I!" said Hansel.

"Indeed!" cried the officer, glancing at Hansel with a sneer. "You're in this gang, too, are you? Well, we won't have to spare *you* those lashes!"

Just then six more men burst open the front door. This new team announced itself as a government agency.

"Mrs. Besintlan?" shouted their spokesman. "You live here alone?"

"Yes, Sir," she replied, her voice a little shaky.

"As I thought!" the man cried sternly. "You haven't been caught out in your treacherous sentiments before, but a few minutes ago you revealed them openly. A microphone is hidden inside of every television set. It cannot be turned down, as can the loudspeakers. Your comments on our noble government"— here, all twelve men saluted again and cried, "Hail Gorbatlani!"— "were heard, recorded, and reported immediately to Central Control. You, madam, will be deported. Our great and noble leader is ever gracious toward women, and has ordered that we spare them the normal lashes. You are to prepare, however, for immediate deportation to Mexatlán. Your belongings will be confiscated by the State!"

"You mean to strip me even of my television set?" asked Mrs.

Besintlan with an ironic smile. "And *must* it be Mexatlán?" she asked—pleading (so the boys thought) rather like Brer Rabbit begging not to be thrown into the briar patch!

"That will be up to you, Madam. To us, all the colonies equally are places of outer darkness!"

Mrs. Besintlan protested—again, thought the boys, in slightly mocking tones, "But I was only voicing what everybody in Atlantis thinks."

"Atlanteans gather daily to sing the wonders of our glorious land, and of our still-more-glorious leader!" cried the spokesman. Again, all twelve men saluted, shouting together, "Hail Gorbatlani!"

"Dissent," the spokesman continued, "even of thought, is not permitted!"

"The people have no rights," thundered a second agent, "not even to their own thoughts! Control is the word. Control! *Control!*"

"Hail Gorbatlani!" shouted all of them again.

"Does this command come down from the crystal?" Donny asked.

"No one has ever *seen* our great Crystal," replied the spokesman. "No one is *allowed* to see it. No one knows what it looks like. Its influence is invisible, but omnipresent."

"But if no one has seen it, how do people even know it exists?" Donny asked.

"They are not *allowed* to question its existence!" cried the spokesman. "Disbelief is unlawful! You are to be shipped off to the colonies!" he declared again.

"What do you mean by outer darkness?" asked Bobby.

"Any land not exposed to the beneficial rays of our great Crystal," was the stern reply, "lives in outer darkness."

"I must say, I'd very much enjoy the 'outer darkness' of Timiş again!" Bobby whispered to Donny.

"I wish we could bring Mrs. Besintlan with us!" lamented Donny. "She's been so kind to us." To Mrs. Besintlan he said, "I'm so sorry we've brought you this misfortune. Now you'll have to leave your home!"

Mrs. Besintlan whispered back, "I've had a job; that's why I've lived here. But I don't really mind leaving."

"Madam," sneered another agent, "you *deserve* the punishment of exile to Mexatlán!"

"I wish we could take her with us," Hansel said to the boys. "But this is only dream time, so I know it can't be done."

"I'm so sorry!" cried Donny, not realizing that their motherly friend had no idea what they were talking about.

"I don't mind going," she said again, provoking more derision from the men. "And I'd *love* to go to Mexatlán!" She whispered to them, "I have a vacation home there, on a high plateau."

"Well, Mrs. Besintlan," said the government agent with heavy irony, "since there are a certain number of fanatics in this noble land who, like you, don't seem to like the way we do things, we'll be happy to have you to join them in their misery." He gave a loud bark of derision.

They bundled Mrs. Besintlan away. The boys and Hansel were handcuffed and roughly conducted to a van, inside of which they were locked and driven off to a police station, where they were hustled into a large room, crowded with many other prisoners of this "enlightened" regime.

"Stand there!" their captors ordered. "We must summon a judge."

After their captors had left, Hansel looked at the boys slyly. "Shall we?" Silently they nodded their heads.

"Oh, guard," called Hansel, "could you please remove these handcuffs a moment? You've got us safe here, and we'd like to relieve ourselves."

"Sure," said a guard. "It can't really matter." He unlocked their handcuffs. The moment he'd done so, our trio tensed and relaxed their bodies, lowered their hands to their sides, inhaled deeply, then scrolled up their time-light spheres around them. As they stood in them prior to disappearing from the scene, they heard an outraged shout, "Hey, what's going on? Where are you going?"

Suddenly the three found themselves on the grass again, outside the time tunnel. Seated there, they reminisced a while about their recent experience.

"I wonder," said Donny, "why those men considered being sent to the colonies such a terrible punishment."

Hansel laughed. "I've learned during my time travels that negativity eats like a stain into all of one's perceptions. When people exclude any place or person from their sympathies, they cease to see anything good in it, or in him. When they exclude a race, or a whole nation from their sympathies, the excluded are no longer considered to have any redeeming features. Even those who were once friends are now outside the pale. Everything about them is from then on dismissed as dark, evil, and contemptible. In the case of the Atlantean colonies, the officials were so convinced that their own way of life was the only possible way that everything else *had* to produce nothing but misery. They avoided facts as a potential source of confusion."

"As I said," cried Bobby, "what a *dry* outlook—on life—on everything!"

Donny added, "It made everything so *bleak*."

"Yes, *bleak*. That's the word!" Bobby cried earnestly.

"Well," said Hansel, "bleak was what we found it, certainly, beneath that outer glamor. No matter how sweet the apple, it had a wormy core."

Bobby, then: "Doesn't it seem sometimes that, the sweeter the apple, the wormier the core?"

"Bobby!" cried Hansel, "you're too young to be a cynic!"

"What's a sync?" asked Bobby.

"A cynic is someone who turns his nose up at everything."

"It makes him sincle," said Donny, smiling.

"Well, I don't turn my nose up at Apfelstrudel—mit Schlag!" cried Bobby enthusiastically.

"*Ya, das ist himmlisch!* (Yes, that's heavenly!)" said Donny, smiling. He then interjected thoughtfully, "But it does seem, from the time-trips we've taken so far, that there's a catch to everything."

"Egypt wasn't so bad," said Hansel.

"True," agreed Donny, "but you said they, too, slipped into black magic later on. That's surely as bad as anyone can get."

"Granted" Hansel responded. "But at least we can improve *ourselves*, by seeing the mistakes others make. Do you suppose the people we see, too, ever get that advantage? Has Vlad, for example, ever had a chance to reform?"

Donny, eagerly: "Yes! Do you suppose they themselves get to come back again and again, learning from their mistakes each time, until they become—Jesus used the word—*perfect*?"

"I wonder," said Hansel.

"But why can't we learn our lessons all at once, and get them over with?" asked Bobby.

"You know you'll have to drink a certain amount of water every month," Hansel replied. "That doesn't mean you can drink it all at once, and get it over with!"

"What a slow journey!" commented Bobby, sadly.

"We'd better get back to the inn," prompted Donny. "Do you suppose Frau Weidi will give us Apfelstrudel—with Schlag, as she did yesterday?!"

"Yesterday! Only think!" muttered Bobby, as they ran into the bushes hiding the time tunnel, and disappeared.

CHAPTER 8

Utopia?

"T LOOKS," SAID DONNY WHEN THEY ALL CAME together the following morning, "as if people keep wanting to create a perfect world, instead of trying to become more perfect, themselves."

"And see how they stumble!" exclaimed Hansel. "There have been many books describing 'utopia' as men called it. *Utopia* was a word in ancient Greek that meant 'no place.' None of those experiments has ever succeeded."

"*Has* succeeded?" asked Donny, "or *have* succeeded?"

"Oh, gee, Donny!" cried his brother. "Can't you leave such questions alone?"

"I'm sorry," Donny said. "But I get confused if things aren't stated properly."

"None means '*not one*,'" said Hansel. "That's why people say '*has*,' after 'none.' You're not talking here of several experiments, but of only one."

"But there *have* been several experiments," Bobby objected, "so why not just say 'have'?"

"You have a point, Bobby," admitted Hansel. "Let's get on and talk about those experiments. Plato, the famous Greek philosopher. . . ."

"What's a fil-suffer?" Bobby demanded.

"A philosopher, Bobby, is someone who *loves* wisdom, but who isn't necessarily, himself, wise. Usually, his so-called 'wisdom' is only theoretical. Plato was a perfect example of what I mean. He tried to box people in with questions, force them in the direction he wanted them to go, and then, like a magician producing a rabbit out of a hat, cry: 'See, your own logic *forces* you to my conclusion!' And people were slow-witted enough to nod, bow, and solemnly declare, 'O wise one, you've beaten us in argument!'

"The trouble is, reason can be used in almost any way one wants. It can herd people like sheep into an already-built pen."

"Yes!" cried Donny. "I've sometimes done that with Mother, just in fun. The other day she gave me spinach, and because I'm not fond of spinach I said, 'Mother! Spinach is *green*, and green is the color of envy and jealousy! You don't want your son growing up envious and jealous of others, do you?' Of course she knew I was joking, and of course so I was! But I do see your point, Hansel."

"Well, many of Plato's theories were very intelligent, but that didn't make them right. Using his method, Plato wrote a famous book, *The Republic*, applying his reasoned approach to the creation of an ideal society. He outlined what he thought would bring about a state of social perfection.

"The governing elite of that society," Hansel continued, "were supposed to live under an almost communistic system, sharing all property, residences, and meals. They were to be allowed free entry into one another's homes. They would live together (whether in one building or in several doesn't seem clear, since he said they could freely enter one another's homes), eat together, and shun every semblance of a family life as distracting to their public service. The ruling classes were not permitted to marry or have mates of their own, and any children they produced were never to be recognized as their own. Children would never know their parents, moreover: all were looked upon as offspring of the State."

"Gee," cried Bobby, "if I couldn't recognize Mother and Daddy, who would there be to love me?"

"Precisely, Bobby!" Hansel answered. "There was no love in that system. Like most of Plato's ideas, it was an intellectual concoction, altogether dismissive of the heart's feelings. That has been the real problem all along with modern science. But still we should ask ourselves, '*Might* it have worked?' Fortunately, that question can be answered.

"In 367 BC, Dionysius the Younger, ruler of Syracuse (in Sicily), invited Plato to come and make his kingdom over into an 'ideal' state along the lines described in *The Republic*. The experiment was a failure.

"We ourselves, however, at this late time in history, can do little more than theorize. So why don't we go back to those times, and see for ourselves what really happened?"

"Oh, do let's give it a try!" cried Donny.

They enclosed themselves in their time-light spheres, and very soon found themselves in the city of Syracuse, in the year 396 BC. They scrolled down their spheres, and walked about the city pretending to be plain citizens like everyone else. Walking along a narrow sidewalk, they encountered a bent old man hobbling, with the help of a cane, in the opposite direction to themselves. This tottering ruin of humanity tried to walk right through them!

"Look where you're going, peasants!" he shouted brusquely.

A nearby policeman shouted at them, "Louts! Don't you know the members of our elite when you see them?" Well, the old man *had*, in fact, been dressed somewhat differently—wearing a long, white robe. Everyone else wore cheap and inelegant clothes.

"They ought to be publicly whipped!" cried the old man. What kind of ruler, wondered the boys, was this? Obviously, people were there to serve *him*, not he, *them*.

Bobby went up to the policeman and said, "Please Sir, we aren't from Syracuse, and I'd like to know: Isn't this supposed to be some sort of *ideal* state?"

The policeman looked down at the little boy and smiled. (Donny thought, He must have children of his own.) "It *is* ideal," he said, "inasmuch as it works quite logically, like clockwork. But the mainspring isn't the people: it's the ruling elite. We're all logical here, and it makes sense for a body to be ruled by the head. The rest of us are only cogs; our role is to help keep the machinery running." The man preened himself a little over the neatness of his simile.

Donny turned to Hansel and said, "Can't we go among the elite, and see what *they're* like?"

"I think that might be a good idea. We'll learn nothing here, and we'll be treated, in addition, only like parts of a machine."

They scrolled up their time-light spheres—noting the fear in the faces of passersby on beholding feet, legs, upper bodies, and heads disappear before their very eyes. In a moment, the three were inside a great hall, where again they scrolled down their spheres. People in long, white robes strode about, hardly glancing at one another, and certainly not acknowledging the existence of our three friends. When anybody met someone he knew, both raised their right fists and shouted, "The State is God!"

One man bumped into a little boy, knocking him over. "Respect for the State, you brat!" he cried, then marched off, leaving the child in tears.

Someone came over, picked up the child, and spanked him on his little bottom. "Don't you know that crying is disallowed here? Respect for the State, brat!"

Other children gathered around the stricken child.

"Crying isn't logical!" one of them scolded. "We need to be guided by cold reason. Feeling is weakness. Feelings must be *suppressed!*"

"So you feel sorry for yourself?" demanded another child mockingly. "Submit a complaint to the senate. They'll hear it in formal court—maybe after three years!" Sneering, he then ran off.

Bobby went over to the little boy. "Where's your mother?" He'd forgotten what Hansel had told them on *that* subject.

"I don't *have* a mother!" lamented the little boy, feeling very sorry for himself. "The State is my mother, my father, my everything. And just see how long it takes to get a hearing from the State!" He began to weep again.

Just then a woman strode up and addressed the three of them. For clothing she wore a long, straight sheath ("probably starched," thought Donny). The whole outfit was a sterile white. "Get that brat back into the official nursery where he belongs!" she commanded. "They'll know how to discipline him there. We've no room for feelings here! Everything must be run in an orderly manner."

"But you produce children!" objected Hansel. "Doesn't it take *some* feeling to want to have children?"

"Nonsense!" the woman cried. "It is nothing but biology. Our feelings are channeled into inviting reasonable children into the State. We mean to stock our nurseries with children who show promise of becoming a responsible ruling elite, as governors of our future."

"And what does this elite do?" asked Hansel.

"Pass laws, of course! A society can be ruled only by law and order."

"But do you yourself never feel anything for anybody?" Hansel persisted.

"I try sincerely not to!" retorted the woman, staring at him grimly. "Feeling only undermines the clarity of logic! We Utopians are determined to make the State all powerful!"

"But *you* aren't the State!" Hansel objected.

"No, I am not!" declared the woman, firmly and proudly. "I am a *subject* of the State. There is no other purpose for my existence. The State is God!"

"But is God the State?"

"There can be no other God *but* the State!" came back the harsh reply.

"Please, Ma'am, we're strangers here," said Bobby.

The woman looked at him as if suddenly seeing him as an individual for the first time. There was no kindness or welcome in her expression, however; she only noted his existence as a cold fact.

"May we visit your home?" Bobby persisted.

"We *have* no homes," she declared almost fiercely, as if repressing something in herself. "We live in dormitories: the women in one set, the men in another. Each group sleeps with its own set, eats with that set, dresses and undresses with that set. Our offices are our homes. In them, we make ourselves useful to the State. We work together in large rooms, the desks touching one another for maximum efficiency in the use of space."

"Well," said Donny, "may we join you for a meal, and ask you a few questions?"

"Nobody talks at mealtimes," declared the woman. "No one is allowed to talk. Talking would be inefficient."

"But don't you at least *enjoy* your meals?" Bobby inquired.

"Enjoyment of any kind is only sentiment," she answered. "We try to eliminate sentiment from our lives altogether."

"But then," Bobby asked, "is what you eat even tasty?"

"We make it as tasteless as possible," the woman declared proudly. "Just wheat and water; no sugar; water to dilute the juices; plain yogurt to stimulate the digestion, but not the palate; meat that has been carefully dried to its essential, nutritive essence; a gruel sprinkled with a little powdered skim milk; a warm drink—never hot—brewed from a few leaves rich in medicinal properties; eggs (hard boiled only), with a pinch of salt to maintain our energy at work."

"Gee, thank you, Ma'am. I think we'll skip that meal for now," said Donny. "Don't you agree?" he asked his companions. Bobby made a clowning gesture behind the woman's back, as if sicking up that once-hoped-for meal.

"Have you seen enough?" asked Hansel. "Shall we go back to our sward?"

"Do let's!" cried Bobby.

"I've had enough of this 'ideal State' to last me lifetimes," Donny said.

"As I told you," Hansel reminded them, "the experiment was a flop. So much for philosophy! We have to do more than *think* our way to truth, and to perfection. We must also *feel* both of them. The mistake people make is to think any mere system can produce perfect human beings. Perfection can be achieved only by perfect people. It must begin in the heart of the individual."

They sought out a hidden corner in that great hall, and there, unseen by anyone striding grandly around them, they scrolled up their time-light spheres, and disappeared. No one even glanced at them; that entire, grim elite were completely intent on pursuing their State-dictated obligations.

Moments later, the three manifested themselves outside the time tunnel, scrolled down their time-light spheres (thus freeing themselves of that hindrance to free movement), and sat down on the grass in comfort.

"What do you think you've gained, Boys, from today's experience?" asked Hansel.

"I think," Donny said, "it may be good to have instruction from someone who knows what he's talking about, but intelligence isn't enough. The teacher must have *experienced* his wisdom for it really to be valid."

"I get the impression," said Bobby, "that people who reason too much consider themselves better than anyone else."

"Isn't it amazing," Donny chimed in, "how many people seem to *need* someone to look down on!"

"Why do you suppose they do that?" asked Hansel.

"I think it's because they feel somehow inadequate in themselves," Donny said, thoughtfully.

"But can't they see," Bobby persisted, "that we're all equal? I mean, yes we have different abilities, but who's to say that any one ability is better than any other? We're just human beings. Age may give us more experience, and more knowledge, but it doesn't necessarily give us more *wisdom*. Look at those *dry-as-dust* grown-ups in Syracuse!"

"I think," said Donny, "I want to live my life *helping* people, not sneering at them, and not using them to make myself more important."

Hansel said, "That desire is a feeling! It would have excluded you from belonging to the ruling elite of Syracuse."

"They didn't even really *want* people to be wise," Donny remarked. "They wanted machines! How can any mere system produce perfect people? To achieve perfection, people need the *incentive* to become perfect. And incentive is a *feeling*. In this case, the incentive toward perfection has to be *love!*"

"But gosh!" Bobby exclaimed, "these outings in time are really *helpful*! Thank you, Hansel, so much."

"I'll see you in *your* tomorrow, Boys. I'll be waiting for you here."

"Yes, Hansel," they both cried. Bobby added, "Oh! this is all so *exciting*!"

In a moment they entered the time tunnel, and returned to their present.

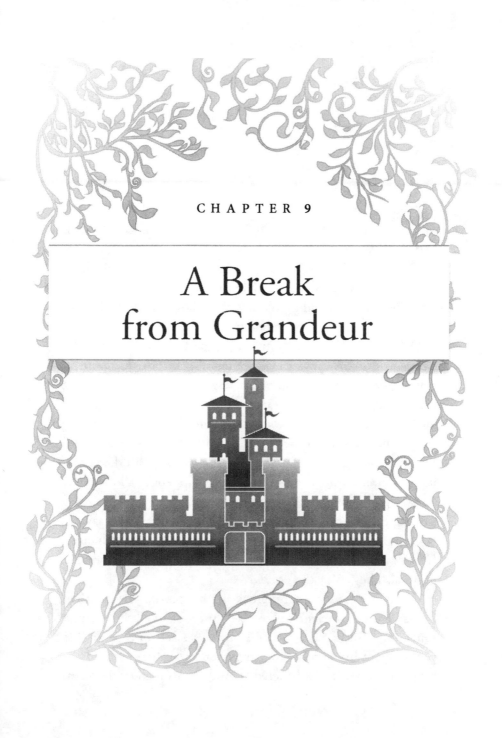

CHAPTER 9

A Break
from Grandeur

**T**HEY MET AGAIN NEAR THE TIME TUNNEL ON THE "sward."

Donny started in right away with an objection. "Why is history all about kings and wars and atrocities and outstanding blunders? Millions of people live on earth. Why can't the history books write about them?"

"Well," said Hansel, "you can't expect those books to be clogged up with things that happen all the time, can you? A newspaper editor once defined a newsworthy story: 'If a dog bites a man,' he said, 'it isn't news. But if a man bites a dog, *that* may be worth printing, because it's *unusual.*'"

"So the wars and other horrible things that happen," said Donny, "are worth putting in history books? But I get the impression that those things, too, keep happening all the time. So why pay all that attention to them?"

"I agree, Donny," Hansel replied. "The French have a saying: 'The more things change, the more they remain unchanged (*Plus ça change, plus c'est la même chose*).' People don't enjoy the unusual. They enjoy the *extreme.*"

"I sometimes wonder if there is anything more perverse than human nature," exclaimed Donny. "Just look at all the peculiar things we've seen: Vlad Dracul *enjoying* his acts of cruelty. (Do you suppose his victims, too, may somehow have *enjoyed* the terror they themselves suffered?!) And then Gessler: He seems to have *loved* challenging William Tell to shoot that apple from his son's head! And then William Tell, himself: I suppose he kept repeating that story for the rest of his life. Why? and why do people enjoy telling it even now? And those people on Atlantis: They seemed to *enjoy* harassing people with their power. And didn't those who objected to the system somehow *enjoy* protesting against it?"

"You certainly have a point, Donny," said his grown-up friend. "People suffer, then tell themselves, 'I don't think anyone can ever have suffered as greatly as I have!' They take pride in that very thought!"

"I sometimes get upset," Bobby chimed in, "but later on I think, Life would be boring if I *never* had anything to upset me!"

"Yes, that's what I mean," said Hansel. "That's *exactly* what I mean!"

"So do people *like* to suffer?" Donny wondered. "It hardly makes sense. It's like scratching a mosquito bite—painful, but at the same time pleasant! Is it *human* nature, or is it just Nature itself? Everything seems two-sided—or is it two-faced?"

"You know," Hansel said, "we could go back to some time when people weren't fighting all the time, or doing the unusual things that got them into history books. We might take a look at ordinary poor people, living ordinary lives, in ordinary circumstances—maybe getting bit by dogs, instead of biting them, and just eking out existence in leaky huts, shivering without heat during cold winters, and wearing little but rags. We might learn something from their lives, too."

"That doesn't sound very exciting," was Bobby's comment. "We've seen enough of poverty already in Romania!"

"In some ways, Bobby," said Donny, "don't poor people seem even to *enjoy* their poverty? Do you remember that time in Bucharest, when we went ice skating, and a group of gypsy children came to us whining, 'We've had nothing to eat for three days!' Well, we gave them a little money, then went in into the skating rink. When we came out, those same children were playing in the street, laughing happily. The moment they saw us, they threw up their hands, excitedly crying, "Ah!" Then they came to us again, whining, 'We've had nothing to eat for *three days!*'"

"Well, but I don't suppose *they* were suffering at all!" said Bobby.

"Well, then," retorted Donny, "they enjoyed mimicking suffering."

"Think of it!" exclaimed Hansel. "There seems to be a kind of happiness in suffering itself! and the opposite is true also: there's a kind of suffering also in happiness—at least the suffering of knowing the happiness can't last! And look at those men in Atlantis!"

"They did seem, in a way, to enjoy their joylessness!" exclaimed Bobby.

"We've at least *seen* poverty," Donny said. "But why don't we go somewhere today—not in this time zone, but back in time to make it more interesting—and see real poverty up close for ourselves."

"As good a time period as any," said Hansel, "might be Normandy during the time of William the Conqueror."

Bobby remarked with rather less enthusiasm, "As long as we can get back to the inn in time for supper!"

"But that reminds me, Hansel," said Donny. "We brought a bag of sandwiches with us today, thinking you might enjoy one."

"I might at that. But might it not help the people we'll be

visiting, if we took these sandwiches to them?"

The boys agreed enthusiastically.

"Back we go, then!" cried Hansel.

Suddenly they found themselves outside a tumbled-down hut. As they unscrolled their time-light spheres, they heard pitiful cries of hunger from within the hut. The time was late autumn, and a cold rain fell steadily. Hansel knocked on the door, and called out, "May we come in?"

"You'll be welcome," replied a kindly voice. "You'll be *more* than welcome if you've brought us food to eat. And you'll be *triply* welcome if you've brought something to seal the leaks in this roof over our heads."

"We do have food for you," Hansel announced. The flimsy door was flung open eagerly, and a woman looked out. Rain, they saw, was dripping through the broken roof in many places.

"Let's see what you've brought!" The woman asked before even welcoming them in. Then, "Come in! I hope the food you've got is all for us, though in these terrible times I know we'll probably get only the crusts!"

As the visitors stepped inside, they found there a thin woman and three children, ranging upward in age from about three years. The woman had a sweet smile, but it also showed a lot of pain.

"My married's in England," she said. Donny and Bobby thought she looked much too old to be having children at all. "He's fighting for Duke William's rights. But here we are alone, cold, and *hungry*! What can I do? It's a challenge just keeping body and soul together."

"We've brought you a little help, Mother," said Hansel. "This whole bag of food is for you!" He gave her all the sandwiches.

Eagerly she seized them, took a bite, then gave the rest to

her children. "I must keep up my own strength," she said, "for their sake." This statement, coming from her, didn't sound self-justifying at all.

"Duke William's cause is just and honorable," she told them. "But it has left many people destitute and starving. What are we to do? The sandwiches you've brought won't last long; they are almost painful to swallow even now, on these empty stomachs, but at least they're food. When you people leave, what shall we do?"

"Why is Duke William in England?" Bobby asked.

"God told him to bring about great changes to the world. England (so my married thinks), being a separate landmass from Europe, can be changed more easily and more permanently. But it's a fearsome task! People insist on clinging to the old ways, even if those ways brought nothing but misery. And all the earls want is personal power. At least Duke William doesn't want power for himself. While he lived here in Normandy, he created a country where learning flourished, and the arts, and religion. He built monasteries, where many men and women served God and worshipped Him. Everything flourished in those times: music; prayer. William wants to bring those good things to England, too—'Angle-land'! land of 'Anglo-Saxons,' where as many heathen Norsemen live as Christian Germans. And the earls—merciful heavens! All they want is to rule, as ruthlessly as they please!"

Donny: "It seems that power is what everybody always wants! *Why?*"

"I don't think Duke William wants power for himself," the woman answered. "When he lived here in Normandy, we saw him attending to the needs of the people. He wasn't looking to be served by them. Still, of course, people who want power for themselves will say that's all William wants, too."

"Do *you* want power?" Bobby asked with curiosity, but not suspiciously.

"*Me?!*" The woman laughed wheezily. "Why would a person like me want power? Could I *eat* it? No, give me enough food for me and my babies, so we can go on living, and I'll have everything *I* want!"

"I'm beginning to think," said Donny thoughtfully, more to Hansel than to the woman, "that, once people satisfy any one of their wants, they only go rushing off in search of something *else* to want!"

"But *power!*" Bobby said. "It seems to me that, if people aren't looking down, they're all wishing they could be 'up there,' looking down. People seem so filled with envy."

"I don't look up," said the woman. "I'm contented with my lot. But something to eat would be nice, and a real roof over our heads."

"To have no ambitions seems worthwhile, in a way," was Donny's comment. "But it seems to me we should all be ambitious at least to do *good*."

"Instead of having good done to us!" was Bobby's addition.

"Why not want to have good done to us?" asked the woman's oldest child, a little snippet about eight years old, but with an old face.

"Why, you ask?" repeated Bobby. "Because giving makes us happier than being given to."

"I'm not so sure about that!" muttered the little one.

"*I'm* sure!" cried Bobby. "But then, I've been around more than you."

"*More* than me? You seem much too little to boast of having done more than me!"

"I've gone to more places, in lots of . . ."

"Bobby!" his brother cried warningly.

"Oh, I forgot!" said Bobby, putting a hand over his mouth. But what he'd said pleased Donny. Evidently, his little brother no longer felt a need to keep harping competitively on his own age. *Something* good, surely, was emerging from their time traveling!

Donny gave Hansel a pleading look. "May we go outside for a moment?"

Excusing themselves to the peasant woman, they stepped out of the hut.

Donny said, "She seems a worthy person. Can you suggest any way that we might help her?"

"Well," said Hansel, "we might find her a position in a nearby castle. But we're not allowed to interfere in other time zones."

After a pause, Donny answered, "But we helped Mrs. Besintlan didn't we, in Atlantis?"

Hansel was very much taken aback. "It's true!" he said. "We changed her destiny. I wonder how we managed that. We broke the rule—yet we did it successfully!"

"I understand!" cried Donny. "She *loved* us! Remember how she confided in us? It must have been love that broke through the time-zone limitation. Love, I think, embraces eternity!"

"By the Great Crystal!" cried Hansel, smiling humorously. "That *has* to be the answer! Love is just the kind of thing that doesn't get written up in lists of rules and laws, or in history books."

"And Mother says that love is the secret of all true understanding!" Bobby added enthusiastically.

"I think we all admire this poor peasant woman," said Hansel, "because she's not only brave, but noble-souled. See how she thinks first of her children. And, though she leads a very hard life, it hasn't made her bitter."

"I think we can say that we love her, too," added Donny.

"So then, surely we can help her!" cried Bobby.

They re-entered the dilapidated hut.

"Madame," Hansel began, "there is something we'd like to do for you. May we go away for a bit, and return? We'll bring you more food."

"By all means come back! I'm so worried about my babies! What if one of them should grow ill?"

"We'll be back very soon, Mother—very, very soon. Have we your permission?"

"As if you needed it!" she laughed. "Most people don't call me 'Madame.' They just point at me and say, 'Hey, you!'"

The three went outside, scrolled up their time-light spheres, and willed themselves to the nearest castle. Before approaching the portcullis, but after unscrolling themselves, they paused a moment. Hansel said, "Where shall we go first?"

Bobby answered, "Why not to the kitchen?"

"The kitchen it is, then!" said Hansel.

They addressed a sentry. "Please, Sir," Hansel began. . . .

"'Please?'" repeated the man, emitting a sharp bark of a laugh. "That word isn't one we hear often in these times! You must be seeking a favor. So what is it. Let's see if I grant it. Shall I?"

Hansel said a little proudly, "I'm here to *confer* a favor! I want to talk to the person in charge of the kitchen."

"In that case, sure!" said the sentry. "We'd be happy for favors in *that* department. See those stairs to the left? Go up them, and ask for Jacques Bondieu."

"Bondieu. Right." The three of them headed up the stairs, Bobby, especially, wearing an air of self-importance. They were going to see an *authority*, after all!

When they met Jacques Bondieu, they found him to be a rotund, jolly person. "What can you do for me?" was his first question, which he gave humorously. He'd heard nothing from them about favors, whether given or received. Evidently, jocularity was his mind-set. Hansel, however, had the formula of his plea already fixed in his mind by that verbal exchange he'd had with the guard.

"I'm here, Sir," he said respectfully, "to tell you that I've just encountered the most fabulous cook! When you eat her confections, you'll be simply amazed at her skill. She's fallen on hard times now, but so also have many others. Still, you'll find she can be a great help to you in preparing banquets for your lord."

"Well," said the jolly man, "we can certainly benefit from such a marvel! Let her come, first. Then we'll see."

"May we bring her back later today? She is nearby, but she didn't want to come unless she was welcome. And may we have a little something to nibble on till we return?"

"Of course!" cried Jacques. "Take this piece of flatbread."

They went back outside the castle walls, scrolled up their time-light spheres, and appeared once again before the woman's hut. Unscrolling themselves, they knocked on the door and entered. The woman was tenderly stroking her middle one's brow, urging him to get some sleep.

"Back already?" she commented. Poverty hadn't made her bitter; she actually smiled, though wincing a little with the effort: her empty stomach gave her great pain.

"Mother," said Hansel, "We've brought you something more to eat." He gave her all the flatbread. "And I've found you employment as a cook! The chef at the castle is waiting to appraise your skills. Can you cook?" He urged her: "Please don't say no: I have told him about your marvelous cooking."

"You have, have you?" The woman chuckled with amusement. "Well, I used to make what my married called a very good stew."

"That'll do!" cried Hansel. "Bring your children, and come with us. By the way, what is your name?"

"Mme. Severin," she replied.

Mme. Severin roused her sleeping children, looked about her for a not-too-ragged shawl to put around her shoulders, and joined them at the door. Miles they walked through the bleak countryside. Mud on the road would have dirtied an aristocrat's clothing just as badly as a peasant's. On arriving at the castle, Hansel said importantly to the guard (he wanted to impress the man, a different one from before), "We have an appointment with Jacques Bondieu." They got in without difficulty, and soon found themselves standing before the chef.

"This, Sir, is Mme. Severin. I've brought her with her children."

"Not much of a specimen, is she!" was Jacques's comment, which he gave with a laugh. "Still, you say she cooks well? These roads are wet and muddy enough to ruin anyone's clothing. Well, Mme. Severin," he said respectfully, addressing her directly. "We have a banquet tonight. Could you make a good stew with which to grace it?"

"*Yes, Sir!*" she replied, speaking with dignity, and trying not to show her pleasure in having this particular dish selected for her first try. The choice, surely, was heaven-sent!

Hansel asked, "Is there some room you can give Mme. Severin to live in? It would hardly do to have her tramping back and forth. . . ."

"Of course! Of course! Come with me, Madame," cried Jacques enthusiastically. They disappeared together briefly.

"Is that luck, or is it luck?" whispered Bobby to his older brother.

"I have a feeling," said Donny, "that luck gets a good prod in the back when people hold positive expectations!"

"Luck also gets a prod from positive *feelings*," said Hansel.

Bobby asked, "You mean, *our feelings* help to determine the outcome of what we do?"

"Of course!" said Hansel. "Everything, as I've already explained to you, is conscious, and an expression of consciousness. Negative thinking blocks any positive flow. If, for instance, you tune in to the *feeling* behind a piece of music, you can produce sounds a thousand times more beautiful than you would if you considered the music only a random assortment of notes. If you want to make war, *think* yourself a good warrior. If you want to paint, *think* yourself a good artist. If you want to make money, *visualize* money pouring into your coffers, and it will do so. And if you want to learn any difficult subject, tell yourself you *love* that subject. If you hate it, instead, you'll never learn it."

Donny said, "Mme. Severin has a noble attitude toward her misfortunes. Desperately poor as she is, it would have been easy for her to become bitter."

"Had she done so," Hansel commented, "she'd never have emerged from poverty as we've helped her to do. People get from life only echoes of their own expectations. Look at those men who loved to exert power over others. If they'd used their power to *help* people, rather than to lord it over them, they'd have found themselves filled with kindness, and they themselves would have been happy. But because they used their power in a negative way, they became cynical, hard, and bitter."

"How does it work, becoming successful through positive thinking?" asked Bobby. "Is it your own thoughts that have that power? It all seems almost magical!"

"Instead," Hansel answered, "what I think happens is that you *tune in* to a much greater reservoir of consciousness. It's like a violin: if you had only the strings to bow or to pluck, the sound would hardly be heard even twenty feet away. But because the wood under those strings augments their sound, the music played on a little violin can fill a large concert hall. So, when you hold positive expectations, the universe itself will support those expectations. But if you question that support, you'll nullify its every influence in your life."

"And if you hold *negative* expectations," Donny asked, "does a negative consciousness reinforce them, also?"

"Absolutely yes!" insisted Hansel. "In all my time travels, I've seen negative expectations produce collapses and failures on a colossal order. Conditions, in themselves, are always neutral. It's what we make of them that makes them, for us, either good or bad, pleasant or unpleasant, beneficial or disastrous. When poor people allow themselves to grow bitter, they attract even more poverty to themselves. A downward-spinning cycle may go on indefinitely, until one tires of forever falling on his nose, and makes up his mind to work his way back to success. All human beings, whether great or small, nobles or peasants, can become heroes if they want to. On the other hand, they can just as equally become failures!"

Madame Severin at last appeared in the kitchen. "Oh, my brave friends, I will ask the good God every day of my life to bless you for what you have done for me and my babies!"

M. Bondieu appeared behind her with a big smile. "The banquet is not for you men, I'm afraid. [Bobby stood a little taller, at this.] I don't do the inviting here! But you can eat the same feast here in the kitchen. I promise you, you'll like it very much!"

Later, when the three friends left the castle, and before they had scrolled up their time-light spheres, Bobby cried enthusiastically, "We gave Mamma Severin our sandwiches, but look what we got in return: a *feast!*"

"And the stew was the best part!" exclaimed Donny.

In their time-light spheres, they re-manifested on the lawn—oh, all right, the *sward!*—outside the time tunnel.

"Look at what happens," Hansel said, "when you confidently expect good things of life—especially when you want to help others."

"There's no one, anywhere," said Bobby, "more important than anyone else."

"They're all given the same opportunities for fulfillment," Donny added. "It all depends on what they *make* of those opportunities!"

CHAPTER 10

Diogenes

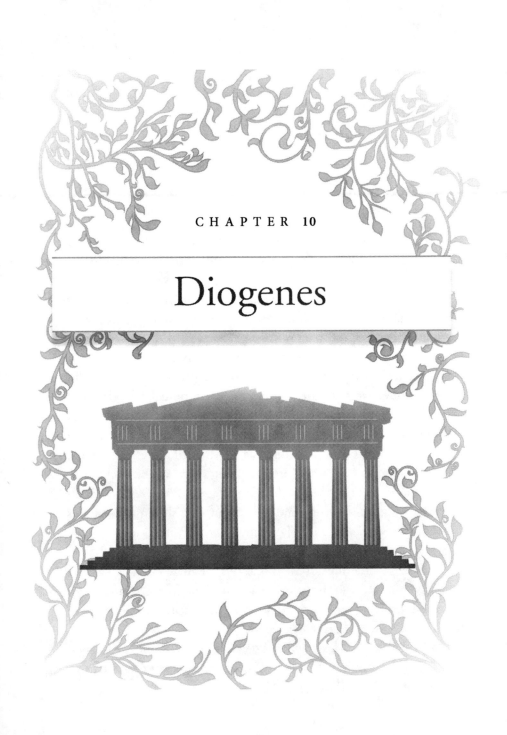

 ASKED YOU, DEAR READERS, AT THE BEGINNING
of my story, whether the events in these pages really
happened. Well, I'm not going to swear they didn't!
But I keep finding myself wanting to put everything
in the present tense, as if everything were happening right now. I
know I'm supposed to keep writing, "He said," and, "They went."
But that's because most books are written about things that have
happened already. What am I to do now, especially if I write about
the future? Must I write, "He says"? or should I say, "He will
go"? or, "He's going to go"? In the present tense it's confusing,
and in the future it's clumsy! And if I put everything in the
present, I don't want to think that Vlad, or the "great and noble
Gorbatlani," could walk into my living room *at any moment*!

In any case, time really exists in the eternal *NOW*. There is no
past or future. Passing time is a dream—an illusion. Even this
time-bridge we call NOW is really only a dream-bridge.

So today—the day after what happened to the boys
yesterday—the three of them find—oh, I guess I must give in to
convention; it's so much easier!—*found* themselves seated once
more, chatting on the sward outside the time tunnel. They were
friends now, and quite relaxed.

"So," Hansel asked, "where do you think we should go today?"

Eagerly Bobby answered, "Well, you *promised* us a trip to
the future."

"And I hope that doesn't mean only tomorrow," Donny chimed in, "or next week."

"Oh, that *would* be disappointing!" cried Bobby. "Even *I* could wait a week to see what happens *then*."

"But if we go farther forward in time," Hansel asked them, "how far would you like to go?"

"That depends," replied Bobby cautiously. "We've seen some pretty gruesome things in the past—though we had some fun back then also!"

"Will we see wars?" Donny asked anxiously, "and bloodshed? and cruelty?"

"Well, certainly there will again be wars in the future, and great suffering, and—yes, cruelty, though most of that cruelty will be refined compared to what we saw Vlad inflicting on those poor peasants. The suffering will also be more intense, for we're living in a time of gradually increasing awareness. The future, for us at this time, means progress, and I'm afraid this means that even the suffering will become progressively more widespread also."

Donny asked, "My daddy said we're now going through a depression—in the world economy. Does that mean there will be other, maybe even greater depressions in the future?"

"I'm afraid so," replied Hansel. "Men will learn, first, how to do things in *big* ways. And that means that they will also *suffer* in big ways."

"What thoughts can we hold during such times," Bobby asked, "so as to suffer in *littler* ways?"

"Maybe," Donny added, "we'll manage not to suffer at all."

"Well," said Hansel reflectively, "I can take you boys back to the time of Diogenes. He might teach you how to cope with lack."

"Who was Diges?" Bobby asked.

"Diogenes was a Greek philosopher. But in this case, his philosophy made him *really* wise. Shall we go there? You might learn something valuable."

The boys assented eagerly. Scrolling up their time-light spheres, they quickly found themselves outside Athens during the time of ancient Greece. To remain invisible, they kept their time-light spheres around them.

A wizened old man was seated before them on the ground, leaning against the tilted bottom of a large wooden basin, long enough for him to lie down in, or *under*, or to lean against on its side-tilted bottom. Diogenes, the old man, was smiling peacefully.

At that moment, a muscular young man appeared before him, elegantly clothed, and accompanied by a large retinue. The youth stood between Diogenes and the sun, himself wreathed in sunlight. His position, however, placed Diogenes in the shade.

"I am Emperor Alexander," announced the youth. He seemed haughty, but there was also a suggestion of sensitivity in his gaze.

Diogenes looked up, smiled, but said nothing. The courtiers, seeing the old man's apparent lack of respect, glanced sidelong at one another and smiled cynically.

"How will the emperor treat this fellow?" whispered one of them.

"Have him whipped, most likely!" the other whispered back.

"I have heard about you," said Alexander to Diogenes, respectfully. "I know you for one of the glories of our empire. I've come here with a wish to reward you as you deserve."

"What has your Majesty to give me?" asked Diogenes.

"I can give you riches! Honor! Public recognition and acclaim! A magnificent mansion to live in! I can make life comfortable for you in your old age."

"And what are those things to me? If there is one thing you can give me, your Majesty, it is something of which you have deprived me: sunlight. You're blocking it. Please step a little to one side."

"You mean, that's *all* you want?"

"What else can I wish? I'm quite comfortable here with my tub. It gives me a bed at night, and shelter in the daytime. If it rains, I can lie down or sit under the tub. If I want a bath, I can pull the tub to the fountain nearby and fill it with water. If I want simply to rest in comfort, I can tilt the tub on its side and lean against it as you see me doing now. People bring me whatever food I eat, and if they bring me nothing I am quite contented not to eat. If I die of hunger, I'll still be at peace. All I want, your Majesty, is peace—peace, and the priceless gift of solitude."

The courtiers muttered together, wondering how the emperor would react, but Alexander stepped to one side obligingly, and smiled with evident appreciation. "Old man," he said, "why do you contemn what others so much crave?"

"I am happy in myself," the old man replied.

Emperor Alexander departed, accompanied by his retinue. He alone, of them all, wore a gaze of respect—and, perhaps also of wonder at this strange experience.

Now here, Readers dear, I encounter a little problem. The Diogenes of history was a controversial old curmudgeon. He is supposed to have done things no truly wise man would have done. But how far can we trust history books? At any rate, *my* Diogenes was a very different man from that one. Maybe there were two men who bore the same name. In fact, quite a few men of that name made it into the history books. And maybe, if my own, *good* Diogenes was the same man I've mentioned, that *true* man may have got slandered by his enemies (as happens very often). People love to spread vicious rumors, and also to listen to them, and are all-too-prone to believe what they hear! One cannot do good in this world without attracting malice.

At any rate, what I'm about to tell you is what really (well, *almost* really) happened to our three friends. After Alexander departed, our three moved before the tub, scrolled down their time-light spheres, and stood facing Diogenes.

"Noble Sir," said Hansel, "we witnessed your unusual encounter with the emperor. Would you mind telling us something?"

Diogenes remained silent.

Bobby, softly to the others: "Do you suppose he heard us? He seems very old. Maybe he's deaf."

"Either that," said Donny, "or he's indifferent."

"I've found, with people of this sort," said Hansel, "that they tend not to waste words. I asked him to tell us something. Perhaps he's just waiting to hear what that 'something' is. Please tell us, Sir," he asked Diogenes again, "can you help us to understand. . . ?"

"I'm happy to help anybody to understand the truth," answered Diogenes, kindly and with respect.

"*That's* a relief!" exclaimed Donny. "I mean, if you can insult your emperor, I wondered what you might do to people like *us*."

"To me," said Diogenes, "you are no different from the emperor."

"A man after my own heart!" exclaimed Bobby.

"What we'd like to know," pursued Hansel, "is how not to let poverty, or sudden loss, or maybe insults or even death, disturb us."

"That," said Diogenes, "is a worthwhile question. It strikes at the root of all human misery. What you must do is realize that you are not yourself."

"Not *myself*! " cried Bobby. "Mother's always telling me to *be myself*, to *act my own age*!"

Diogenes smiled calmly. "I don't mean *that* self. I can see that this tall fellow beside you has already explained these things to you. What I mean is that everything is made of consciousness."

"But I still don't understand," complained Bobby. "A table is made of wood. That's a *thing*. But consciousness isn't a thing. How can anything be made of the nothing that is *consciousness?*"

"What is your name, young man?" asked Diogenes.

Bobby preened himself a little on hearing himself addressed as a man. "I'm Bobby," he replied. "And this is my brother, Donny."

"Well, Bobby, think of the substance of everything as being like an ocean with many waves. The waves, like the ocean, are made of water; in fact, they're made of the *same* water. But each wave is different in appearance, and they all change their appearances constantly."

"I can understand that," said Bobby. "Yet the waves aren't solid."

"But they do have substance," countered Diogenes. "So also does air. And though Aristotle says air is nothing, you've seen birds fly: they certainly are supported by *something*. Consciousness, too, though you can't touch it or feel it (as you can water), obviously exists. You yourself are conscious; *you* know that's true, even if strangers, seeing you asleep, might question whether you are really conscious at all."

Hansel interrupted: "I know that some people claim that thoughts are only moving energy in the brain. But even if that is so, it doesn't explain *consciousness*."

"Obviously not," said Diogenes. "Your consciousness, like the ocean, only *manifests* thoughts. Those thoughts are like waves. The ocean doesn't create waves: it *manifests* them."

"Gee," said Bobby, "this is *heavy!*"

"Not really," Donny countered. "You dream because you are

conscious, don't you? If you weren't conscious—if you were just a stone, for example—you wouldn't dream at all; you wouldn't be able to dream. In your dreams, you may see solid-seeming objects, but they are only your mental creations."

"Each ocean wave," continued Diogenes, "has its own shape, and rises to its own height. The larger the wave, the more likely is its size to obscure the fact that it really is only a bulge on the surface of the ocean."

Bobby: "I'm struggling, but I'm still afloat!"

"But yes, I *see*!" cried Donny. "We aren't waves, but we do change. We grow bigger, we become stronger, then we grow old; in the end, we become feeble, and then die. But is even death the end?" To Diogenes: "If we sink back into the ocean like spent waves, do we lose our individuality? Do we just become re-absorbed—indistinguishable from the rest of that body of water?"

"No, we don't," answered Diogenes. "Our single, coherent thought, 'I am a self, temporarily defined by a body,' stays with us when we leave our bodies. Thus, we retain our individuality."

"Whew!" Bobby exclaimed. "That's a relief!"

"But it ought *not* to be!" Diogenes declared, with a mock expression of sternness.

"Why not? I remember a nightmare I once had," Bobby persisted, firm in his opinion. "When I awoke from it, I remember what a *huge* relief it was! 'I'm really here again,' I thought, 'in my own bed, and Daddy and Mother are in the next room. I'm *safe*!'"

"It was the safety of a chicken in its coop!" commented Diogenes as relentlessly as Bobby, but with a quiet smile, "A chicken held there against the time when it will be cooked and eaten!"

"Oh, dear!" cried Bobby. "What you're saying is more frightening than any nightmare!"

"Not really," said Diogenes reassuringly. "There is self-awareness in every drop of the *conscious* ocean water. You, one little drop in the ocean, will always remember that you have been Bobby, and you'll be able, from that memory, to relate to your brother as Donny. Thoughts, you see, never actually die. They, too, are *things*. In the ocean, you won't lose your self-awareness, for in omniscience you'll never lose the thought of that separate *memory*. I find it easy to accept everything calmly, because I know that my own central reality can never through all eternity be damaged, altered, or destroyed."

"So what you're telling us," Donny said, "is that we need to see our reality as a part of the vast ocean of consciousness around us."

"Exactly so," said Diogenes. "What importance, in the end, have individuals—be they emperors or slaves? They're all the same 'ocean water.' For myself, although I love everybody, I need nothing from anyone."

"Then, is the ocean's awareness more a state of clear reason, or of clear feeling?" asked Donny. (This question would remain important for him in the years to come. On some level he knew the answer, but still he questioned.)

"Feeling," replied Diogenes, "is the essence of consciousness. In reason, one watches; in feeling, one is both absorbed and absorbs. In reason, there is no joy; in absolute feeling, on the other hand, there is perfect bliss. Wisdom is a combination of clear reason and clear feeling. Bliss is the essential nature of consciousness, when it is fully aware. Consciousness is self-aware, eternal, changeless, but at the same time, refreshingly ever-new. In that state, one need not do anything, for what he had to do he has already done. One feels no need to say anything, for what he had to say he has already said. He is complete in himself.

"If I can be useful to others, I am happy to be so," continued Diogenes. "Otherwise, I have no need to say or do anything. I love all, but in that love I feel no sense of *need*."

"Do you love even evil people?" asked Bobby, remembering Vlad and Gessler.

"It isn't their evil I love, of course," replied Diogenes. "What I love is their potential—inherent in all beings—for attaining bliss."

"But if you love only people's potential," Donny asked, "do you then not love them also, individually, as human beings?"

"Being human myself, I naturally feel a deeper affinity with that potential in human beings than with the same possibility in a cockroach! I love the *upward* tendencies in everyone, but not the *downward*, evil tendencies. I am like a lyre: as it is played, so does the music sound. Sometimes, indeed, there is intervention from a higher level of awareness, and the lyre is plucked as if by someone else entirely.

"Well," Diogenes added kindly, withdrawing into himself. "Take what I've said in whatever way you like. Your understanding will develop over time."

Not another word could they get out of him. The sage simply sat there, with eyes closed.

"He *is* rather old," said Donny. "Let's not bother him any further."

They re-entered their time-light spheres.

"Would you like to see a little of ancient Greece while we're here?" asked Hansel. "It was a glorious time, historically."

"We were at the Acropolis two years ago," said Donny, "and also saw the Parthenon. I've also read about them in school. Do let's go there again."

"Instantly!" replied Hansel. In fact, hardly a moment later they found their time-light spheres hovering above the fresh, new, and beautiful structures of the Acropolis. They entered the Parthenon in their light spheres, and marveled at the skill that had produced those magnificent statues.

After looking about them for a time with smiles of amazement, Hansel said, "Would you like to see this same scene today?"

"Well," replied Donny, "as I told you, we did go there with our parents last year. It was on our return voyage to America."

"Let's just take a peek," said Hansel with a quiet smile. They fast-forwarded to 1935, still in their time-light spheres, and watched as a group of tourists came out of the Parthenon. They were American.

"And so," one of them was remarking, "I told Amy she ought to finish college. She'd get a better job that way, and she might find a better husband than that shaggy fellow, Jake, she's been going with. Yuk!" The voice faded out as their group moved away.

"Just think!" said Bobby, "After seeing all that beauty, they can exit from that glorious temple talking only of people back home, of their empty lives and empty minds! If such people were to time-travel back to the birth of Jesus, I suspeck—suspect [he corrected himself carefully] they'd ask the Three Wise Men if they'd brought with them a bag of hamburgers!"

"Yet the gold and other things they actually did bring probably symbolized an infinitely more precious food: Love!" said Donny.

They returned in their time-light spheres to their "sward." Sitting there briefly, Donny remarked, "I've always had the impression that truly wise men were indifferent to everybody. But I see now that their aloofness is only a seeming. What they really are is free from any attachments."

"Yes," said Hansel, "but they really do love everybody. They are at peace with themselves, because they need nothing from anyone. In themselves, however, they are completely childlike."

"But somehow," interjected Bobby, "Diogenes didn't seem a bit like me, and I'm a child."

"That's because, though childlike, he wasn't child*ish*," Hansel explained. Bobby began to assume an indignant look, until Hansel added, "He holds no expectations of anything or anyone."

* * * * * *

Later that day at the inn, the boys were seated for supper. They'd had a quick dip in the brook.

"Here is some special bread I made, *with honey*!" Frau Weidi whispered as if confidentially, her motherly face wreathed in a kindly smile.

"Maybe I shouldn't have any," Bobby whispered to Donny. "I'd like to be calm and unruffled, like Diogenes."

"Diet gems?" queried Frau Weidi, overhearing him. "Is that a breakfast cereal? But you're too young to think about dieting!"

"Oh dear!" said Bobby. "No, perhaps you're right. I'll gladly have that bread and honey. Thank you, Frau Weidi!"

"I didn't want to hurt her feelings," he whispered to Donny.

So then, off they went to bed, eagerly anticipating the next day's adventure.

CHAPTER 11

Forward HO! to a Glorious Future

"T LAST, IT'S TIME TO SOAR OFF TO THE FUTURE!"
Hansel said to them. "What do you suppose we'll
see?"

"Well," said Donny, "I imagine we'll see very
highly developed cities, as we saw on Atlantis, and all sorts of
scientific marvels."

"But Atlantis, remember, fell because it was *too* scientific.
It tried to work *against* Nature." Hansel smiled. "Of course,
nobody can work against things as they really are, but Atlanteans
were addicted to the power of reasoning. That led them to think
they had done and always would do everything themselves. So,
then, do we think man will see himself *forever* as competing
with Nature?"

"Oh, I hope not!" cried Bobby.

"As it happens, the future we'll be seeing is much better—and
very different from what you've imagined. Let's go very slowly.
That way, you'll catch a glimpse of other time zones on the way."

They enclosed themselves in their time-light spheres,
and moved forward fairly slowly through time. First, passing
fleetingly before their gaze, they saw widespread poverty, hunger
(even starvation), and rioting. Mobs attacking grocery trucks.
People in the inner cities, altogether bereft of food.

Hansel commented, "It was greed for money that brought on
all this suffering."

The scene changed. High, strange-looking clouds formed by exploding atom bombs rose into the sky on all sides around them.

Hansel commented, "One bomb dropped led to thousands more. Tens of thousands of atomic weapons had been stockpiled. But you boys won't know about those weapons until you're a few years older."

Suddenly a great body came from outer space. It hit the earth with a terrific impact, sending vapor clouds high up into the atmosphere. Clouds covered the entire earth, causing the planet almost to stagger under the blow.

Planet Earth at last emerged once again from under those clouds. The great cities that once had covered the earth were no longer to be seen: *all of them* had been destroyed!

Hansel said: "It seems terrible! It *will be* terrible. But if you think that, in a hundred years, nearly everyone on earth today will be dead anyway, you get the kind of perspective Diogenes was trying to give us. Life goes on. Consciousness goes on. In the end it's all a dream anyway."

They saw little villages springing up, almost like mushrooms, consisting of many different-styled, graceful dwellings.

"Ooh!" cried Bobby. "May we stop here?"

"I thought we might go even further—thousands of years into the future. Would you like to speed up? We can come back here later."

"All right," said Donny. "You decide."

All of a sudden, passing time became a sequence of rapidly changing scenes; then a blur of colors; then, only white space.

Suddenly they slowed, landing on a flowery meadow. Scrolling down their time-light spheres, they stepped out (so to speak) onto that meadow and looked about them happily, inhaling a wonderful combination of scents. The weather was balmy. A soft breeze played as if on harp strings over long meadow grass, creating as it did so delightfully energizing sounds, within which subtle melodies seemed to play.

They noticed that their own bodies seemed lighter, almost airy. Everything around them was graceful. Even the trees grew gracefully. And the hills nearby seemed to have been somehow molded into harmonious shapes.

The colors of the whole scene, too, were enchanting. The flowers on the meadow were many hued, as though someone had chosen them specifically for their variety. The colors they displayed, moreover, were brilliant—shining as if with an inner light of their own.

The blossoms on the trees seemed meant to grace the landscape the whole year around, for many of the trees, whether blossomed or not, were the same species.

A beautiful horse ran about freely in the meadow. After making several turns about the periphery, it trotted over to Donny, butted him playfully, ran off, then came back and nudged him—all this playfully, with obvious affection.

"Look!" cried Donny. "It wants to make friends with me!"

Bobby felt a nudge on his shoulder from behind. Looking back, he saw a large wolf. But before he could cringe away in fear, the wolf raised a paw as if wanting to shake hands! It then lowered its head, and fondly licked Bobby's hand.

"Look," cried Bobby, "I, too, have a new friend!"

A little bird flew down and landed on Hansel's shoulder. It nibbled his ear lightly, as if in friendship.

"Why, *hello*, little friend!" cried Hansel. The bird flew off, then moments later returned, bringing in its beak a worm, which it gave to Hansel.

"Now, what am I to do with this tidbit?" asked Hansel humorously, stroking the little bird's feathers with affection. "I don't want to hurt my friend's feelings!" The restless creature solved the problem for him by flying off again. Hansel surreptitiously dropped the unoffending worm into the tall grass.

Now, here's a problem—an author's dilemma, though this time not a big one. I could of course go back and amend it, but here we are in timelessness: what is there even to go back to? What I forgot to say was this: The boys had brought an extra sandwich with them in their little bag, as they'd done when they visited Mme. Severin. They'd persuaded Frau Weidi to make it for them, not saying it was for Hansel, and she'd started to question them about it, and then had let the matter rest. (After all, she had other things to think about in *her* NOW.)

My dilemma is that I didn't tell you about these sandwiches earlier. Shall I go back and insert them in the story? I think it would impede the action to do so.

So then, all I can say is that, with their bag of three sandwiches, they now sat on the grass beneath a graceful tree and ate them. Surprisingly, no ants disturbed them as they ate. Insects were present, of course, for insects, though inconvenient to human beings, are necessities here on earth, where the ecological balance has to be maintained. The ants, however, and for that matter all the insects around them, never disturbed our friends. Throughout their visit the trio weren't bothered by even a single mosquito!

"I've read somewhere," Hansel said, "that mosquitoes are the material manifestation of human unkindness."

"And unkindness, certainly," said Bobby, "causes at least as much suffering as diseases like malaria."

Their brief repast finished, they stood up. At just that moment a visitor appeared. He was tall, dignified, apparently middle-aged, draped in a long blue robe, the material of which was soft and seemed very comfortable.

"Welcome, Friends!" the man announced with a kindly smile. "I thought I would wait until you'd finished your meal."

"But—how did you know we were here?" asked Donny in astonishment.

"I wasn't spying on you!" the man chuckled.

"Then did you just happen to see us with a telescope?" Bobby asked.

"Instruments are material extensions of man's own mental powers," said their visitor, "whether it be the power to see, to hear, or to accomplish anything he wants to do. When a person develops those powers in himself, he then can command them by the mere power of thought."

Hansel commented, "That doesn't seem so 'mere' to me!"

"True," said the other, chuckling. "But when you've perfected yourself, instead of seeking to create perfection outwardly, these powers appear in you automatically.

"But now come with me," he continued. "I'd like to show you where I live—and, perhaps more to the point, *how* I live. You may find this visit helpful to you, as you go on with your romps through time." He smiled with kindly amusement. "I'm not laughing at you," he added more seriously. "Rather, I'm laughing *with* you! All experiences can prove helpful if we use them wisely. And I do think you're coming through your experiences remarkably well.

"By the way," he added politely. "My name is Satyan. We don't bother with last names here. May I know your names?"

They told him. He then led them to the edge of the meadow, where, within a circle of tall trees (and therefore, at first, invisible to them), they saw a perfectly charming little house. The building, single-storied, was perfectly round. On the outside, surrounding it, stood a graceful row of smooth, white pillars, within which a narrow covered walkway encircled the building.

The house itself was faced on the outside by gleaming white walls. Large windows—of the type we call "picture," though in fact they were considerably larger than the picture windows we know—revealed nothing from the outside, but from within one could relax without being seen from outside. When they went indoors, however, they found they could look out of the windows with no obstruction of any tint of color.

Were the windows even made of glass? The visitors studied them carefully, at first from the outside, then from within, but could see in them no reflection: it was as though the house hadn't windows at all!

"Aren't you concerned lest people in the house bump against these panes and get hurt?" asked Bobby.

"Oh, we sense such things," their host replied casually. "No one in our time zone ever gets hurt."

As they approached the front door, the boys wondered how it would open, for it had no latch. Surprisingly, their host reached out with his left hand, keeping the palm downward, and made a lowering gesture. Simultaneously, the door sank out of sight into the ground. They entered without any obstruction.

"It's a marvel," said Hansel, "but aren't you concerned that a thief might use that simple method to stroll in rather than break in, and take what he wants?"

Satyan smiled. "In our time zone, no one would even *think* of stealing! But even if it were to happen, he'd be perfectly welcome to take whatever he wants."

"I *like* this time zone!" said Hansel.

"Is that how the windows work, too—with a simple gesture?" asked Bobby.

"Of course," their host answered. "Why push them out into the walkway, where they'd obstruct people walking by, or inward into the room, where they'd obstruct movement within the house? This way is much easier, and more harmonious." He reached out, again with his left palm turned downward, and all the windows sank out of sight into the wall beneath them. Visually they could see no difference whether the windows were closed or open.

After letting them enjoy the effect of the open windows for a few moments, Satyan continued, "The weather's so clement here that I rarely close the windows anyway. I did so today only to give you the pleasure of seeing them, and seeing how they work. For I knew you were coming, and knew that the state of dreaming in your time zone necessitates heavy locks and bolts on every outside door."

He led them into the house. The living room had no plushy furniture, but when Bobby sat down on a seemingly hard chair to test it, he cried, "Why, it's *soft*!"

Donny sat on a rather firm-looking couch, and, like Bobby, cried out, "It's—it's so *comfortable*! I don't sink into it at all; it supports me, but the support it gives me—well, I can only call it *friendly*!"

"It yields at every point to pressures in your body," Satyan said, "The result is, you feel almost as though you were sitting on air."

"You have beautiful designs on the floor," Hansel commented, "and though the floor isn't carpeted, I find that it yields slightly to the pressure of my feet! How is that?"

"You see," said Satyan, smiling, "that makes it easier to walk on. But dust can be removed from the room effortlessly."

"May I see how?" Hansel asked.

"Surely," said their host. "First, we'll have to step outside the room for a moment."

They did so; Satyan then explained, "Some things in this house yield to voice commands. Watch: First, we'll close all the windows." To do so, he used his right hand this time, gesturing with the palm upward, raising his hand slightly. Simultaneously, the windows in the room rose silently from below, and closed themselves tightly. "Then we'll close the door to the room," said Satyan. He made the same gesture, again with his right hand, and a window-like panel rose from the floor. Satyan then called out: "Dust!"

Suddenly, through openings along the base of the walls (which his guests hadn't noticed before), there came a sound of wind. Whatever dust there was on the floor (though the guests had in fact seen none) was sucked out of the room and became dispersed outside.

After a moment, Satyan opened the door with a lowering gesture of his left hand. The opening cleared, and they stepped again into the room.

"Well," said Hansel, "but even though there are no carpets to stain, stains do get onto the floor. How do you remove those?"

"Shall we leave the room again?" Satyan asked politely.

After closing the door behind them, he cried out, "Scrub!"

Suddenly a bright orange light appeared over the whole floor. It seemed to pulsate for a moment. Then Satyan cried out, "Clean!" Water suddenly welled up from everywhere on the floor, and was sucked out of the house by the same process that had first cleared the room of dust.

"Fantastic!" cried Hansel. "May we go into the room again now?"

"Of course," Satyan replied, smiling with dignity, and gestured downward with his left hand. The door opened, and they entered the living room again and sat down, the boys on chairs, Hansel on the sofa.

"What about those patterns on the floor?" asked Hansel. "They look like carpets, but obviously they aren't. How did you produce those beautiful designs?"

"If you'll look closely," Satyan replied, "you'll see the patterns are formed by dim lighting underneath. I can change the patterns any time I want to. I can also change the colors."

"Where did you get the patterns?" Bobby asked.

"They exist objectively in Nature. They can be selected and reproduced energetically. Different patterns affect the mind— intellect as well as feelings—differently. This pattern, for instance [he sang the word, "Peace!"], has a soothing effect."

Suddenly, a calm blue color appeared, patterned with what seemed like "swirls" of paler and deeper blue lines, with touches of white and violet.

"This one is for when I want to think deeply." Satyan sang out the word, "Calmness!" Immediately, a calm, indigo color appeared in the oblong where there would otherwise have been a carpet. This pattern was more circular: a whirlpool of light seemed to draw the mind inward.

"This next pattern," continued Satyan, "is for when you have guests and want to be convivial."

This time, he sang out the word, "Friends!" A bright but soft yellow tint appeared. Lines and divers shapes streaked through the pattern in cheerful reds, oranges, and greens. The shapes contained graceful, wavy lines, some of which suddenly broke off sharply at new angles and moved in fresh directions. But when I say they broke off, I don't mean the lines themselves moved. The patterns were stationary. The lines seemed to be in motion because they were so much a part of the mood they created. Many of the lines of this pattern were also curved, with inward dips toward the center of the "carpet," and the two sides of the curves moving outward from that center. The effect of those curves was to induce communication with others, rather than to make the mind too absorbed in its own thoughts.

For a few minutes they enjoyed looking at a variety of

patterns. Then Satyan returned to the "convivial" pattern, and spoke again.

"You remember what I told you under that tree?" he said. "I mentioned that all powers are mental, and exist within ourselves. We don't need instruments to objectify them. Yet I freely confess to a fascination with gadgetry. I was once, myself, a scientist."

"When?" asked Bobby, wide-eyed with astonishment.

Satyan looked at Bobby in silence for a moment, then changed the subject. "I don't really need all the gimmickry I've gathered here, you know. I'd be perfectly happy just sitting and sleeping out of doors under a tree. Bliss, however, is the underlying reality of everything, and creativity is the very nature of bliss. So also is self-expansion. For someone with a taste for it, why not, while still in this physical body, enjoy life according to that nature? Life was never meant to be a grim thing, endured in stern self-denial. It was meant to be enjoyable—even *fun*! And in fact you can only really *enjoy* life when you've risen above every attachment.

"Shall we go into the kitchen? You may like what's there."

They got up and entered a room where they beheld a stove, a countertop, a sink, a refrigerator. What new marvels, they wondered, awaited them *here*? At first, after the time they'd spent on Atlantis, the kitchen in this time zone disappointed them a bit. The stove heated food by radiation from below, rather than by the application of heat, but otherwise it didn't seem terribly fancy. They entered the refrigerator by a door in the wall, and found it well stocked with fruits and vegetables.

"No meat?" asked Bobby.

"No," Satyan answered. "We try not to kill anything here. We've also found it more healthful not to eat meat. In fact, however, one has to kill vegetables, too, when one eats them. One does so either by chewing or by heating them. So it isn't so much the killing that we consider wrong as the willingness to inflict pain. There is no such thing as death. When we cook anything, even lightly, we kill it, but the consciousness in vegetables is less ego-centered than it is in animals. Growing things derive a certain fulfillment from being useful to others."

They came out of the walled-in refrigerator.

"What keeps it cold in there?" Donny asked.

"It can be programmed that way," answered Satyan casually. "The light inside is a chilly blue color. No heat comes from it. In fact, the light itself can be made either warm or cold depending only on the energy activating it. Some energies are cold; others are warm, and even hot. Everything depends, ultimately, on energy, which is much subtler than matter. If the vibrations produced by that energy are very slow, the resulting temperature in the material world is cold. If those vibrations are rapid, the temperature becomes heated. It's all quite simple.

"Warming and cooling trends on earth depend to a great extent on mental vibrations. In many cases, the vibrations themselves are produced by thoughts. When people's thoughts are harmonious, the climate itself becomes mild. When their thoughts are violent—as they have been sometimes in the past—the climate itself grows turbulent: The earth has extra-cold winters, extra-hot summers—or, sometimes, hot winters and cold summers—apparently without a reason. And the earth may become violent, spewing forth hot lava from its interior and creating great earthquakes, which in turn lead to huge tidal waves. Other signs of the earth's displeasure appear; the earth may sometimes resemble a dog shaking fleas off its coat."

"Satyan," said Bobby, gazing out through the open kitchen window onto the garden outside, "what about insects? Don't you worry about them entering through those open windows into your kitchen, and maybe spoiling the food?"

"Well, you see," Satyan replied, "when man's own vibrations are integrated and clear, insects don't enter his vibratory field. They have their own field, as we have ours. Insects maintain a distance from us, not because we deliberately exclude them, but simply because their life passes in a different vibratory region. We may be sitting on the grass with insects flying or crawling all around us, but they keep to themselves even as a rainbow separates light into distinct bands of color."

"So that," said Donny in amazement, "is why the ants under that tree didn't come near us while we were eating! I wondered."

"And birds are able to fly," Satyan added, "not only because flight makes their bodies lighter than air, but because birds are compatible with the vibrations of air, as man is compatible with the vibrations of earth, and fish with the vibrations of water. Birds have a very light, happy vibration. Still, man has developed the consciousness of being able to rise through every vibration, and unite his soul with non-vibrational timelessness."

"This is all great fun!" exclaimed Bobby. "Not that I understand a word of it, but I'm enjoying it *hugely!*"

"Would you like to see more of the kitchen?" Satyan inquired.

"Oh, *yes!*" cried Bobby.

"Here is a mixing bowl. Vibrations of subtle light blend everything together.

"There's a sink over here," he continued, "with hot and cold running water—more or less like what you have in your own time zone. The water doesn't need to be filtered for drinking, however, since our brooks are perfectly clean; they do any necessary filtering by simply not becoming polluted. Instead, they run over clean sand and pebbles. The sink itself is kept clean by vibrations of light."

Satyan, focusing his thoughts, whispered softly, "Clean!" The same orange light they'd seen in the living room suddenly pulsated on all sides of the sink. The material from which the sink was made seemed to pulsate with that light.

"Well, what else can I show you?" asked Satyan. "The gadget we use for eating is highly sophisticated, though it's only as new as our bodies. It is called a mouth, and has a movable jaw and a set of what we call teeth." He smiled engagingly.

Bobby, who was expecting some new marvel, paused a moment, puzzled. Then he smiled. "Oh, I get it!" He laughed happily. Satyan smiled too, with quiet dignity.

"Let me show you the bedroom," he said.

They went into the room, and saw nothing there but a grass mat on the floor. Bobby looked at Satyan questioningly.

"I need no gadgets to help me sleep," Satyan told him. "I simply withdraw my energy from the senses and leave this body—which I never think of as my own. Whether I sleep or not is purely a matter of inclination. I may roam about freely in other realms, as you've been doing through time, or I may rest here quietly in superconsciousness."

To Hansel, Donny said, "Is that what you were speaking about when you described the heightened consciousness in ancient Egypt?"

"I'm not sure," Hansel answered. He asked Satyan, "Is it?"

"The more one approaches the top of a pyramid," Satyan said enigmatically, "the closer everything is to everything else.

"Would you like to see something of our society?" he asked, again changing the subject.

"We'd love to," said Donny, "if you'd care to show it to us."

"Why not?" asked Satyan with a smile. "We don't get many visitors here from other time zones."

"First of all," asked Bobby, "What country is this, anyway?"

"Oh, we no longer have countries!" Satyan replied. "We've dropped all self-definitions such as: 'I'm an American; I'm a

Romanian; I'm a man; I'm a woman.' Loyalty is a virtue, but
not if we let it define us. I am loyal to my mother, though she
died many years ago, and if the occasion demanded it, I would
defend her name with energy. Loyalty to her, and to my friends,
is something I strongly believe in. That doesn't mean, however,
that I define myself as 'the loyal type.' I am loyal because I think
it is right to be loyal; it has nothing to do with my personality.
And, too, our loyalty to any place, cause, or person should
be *deserved!* All of us are simply waves on the sea of infinite
consciousness. That's all the self-definition we need."

They entered an area where the people they saw—there
weren't many of them—spoke little to them, but greeted them
with calm, kindly smiles. They also saw a number of small
houses, some of them *very* small, some of them larger. The
peculiar thing about all of them was that each was different.
Satyan's home had been elegant. Many of the homes they now
saw were hardly more than huts—not hovels, however, for they
were neat, clean, and, though starkly simple, quite attractive.

Some of them, however, were so simple as to be constructed
only of grass, with bamboo poles to give them structural integrity.
The climate was, after all, balmy. The only thing the residents
really needed, if they desired anything, was protection from
the rain. "And even the rain," Satyan said with a smile, "can be
prevented from touching us if we exert a little mental power."[1]
Otherwise, insects were not a problem. Cold and heat were not a
problem. A man could survive happily with nothing more than a
loincloth around his waist. Food? Well, fruits and vegetables grew
in abundance: all a person had to do was go out and pick them.

---

* A Mrs. Sharma, wife of a medical doctor, told me in 1962, in the village of Lohaghat
in the Himalayas, that she had once been in the jungles with her guru (spiritual teacher)
and a small group. Suddenly it rained heavily. The rain fell all around them, but they
themselves remained dry.

Some of the houses, however, were artistic oddities. Instead of the elegant pillars our friends had seen around Satyan's home, some of the residences were built with great blocks of stone—like miniature castles; some were made of adobe. Some had no windows, but only small openings that allowed the air to enter from all sides; some, again, had only *very* small openings—not even windows, really—through which almost no air passed. Some of the houses were constructed of wood frames and plaster. Some were made of marble. Some were entirely of wood. In the matter of color, too, the homes displayed great variety. The one universal feature of the color of those homes was that they were all light and, as it were, pure. No dark or heavy hues could be seen anywhere; black was entirely absent. So also were gray, brown, and beige.

"Why is there so much individual expression in these homes?" Donny asked. "I should have thought, if people wanted to rid themselves of all their self-definitions, they'd want especially to rid themselves of anything that made them unique."

"But don't you see," said Satyan, "each person, in his inner Self, *is* unique! The underlying reality of everything is bliss, but that bliss is ever new, ever interesting, ever special. Every atom is invested with individuality. And Bliss is God!"

"The minister at our church," Donny interjected, "says that God is love."

"Love also," said Satyan, "but love is bliss in action. Bliss is that aspect of love which wants nothing for itself, which thinks only of giving. Such, we are learning here, is our *underlying* reality! That bliss—again, in every atom—is *self*-aware. In its self-awareness, everything is unique. Everyone on earth is seeking—though for the most part unconsciously—his own special path to bliss, and his own unique expression of that bliss.

That is why man, in his ego, tries in different ways to stand out above all others."

"And what is ego?" was Donny's next question.

"Ego is bliss attached to the body. And so," Satyan continued, "people who think themselves unique in the sense of having a separate, individual body and personality try to emphasize their uniqueness by piling up self-definitions like heavy blankets—quilts, eiderdowns, bedspreads!"

"I've always felt a little proud of being an American," was Donny's comment.

"Well, but ask yourself, *Why* does that make you proud?" said Satyan. "If your loyalty as an American is something you consider *right* and just, that is one thing. One should always be loyal to whatever good has been given him by life. But if you consider loyalty as defining your personality, you make it a *self*-definition, which you will then project outward—perhaps in competition—onto others, dividing the Americans from the French, the Germans, the Romanians. Ego is always divisive."

"That's true," Donny replied. "I've seen that it keeps making me compare Americans with the people of other countries."

"People used to say, 'Comparisons are odious.' But they aren't so if you're only trying to deepen your understanding. How else can you reason clearly? You *have* to make comparisons! To make unflattering comparisons, however, based on your own self-definitions: *that* is odious."

"What is ojus?" Bobby piped up, inevitably!

"A thing is odious," said Satyan, "if it is hateful. But we're talking here of self-definitions. People who compare themselves with others usually want to emphasize how *different*, and (usually) how much *better*, they are than everyone else! The problem is, however, that self-definitions make a person *imitative*, not original! If you define yourself as an American, you have to act as you imagine Americans act. If you define yourself as a man, or," with a smile for Donny and Bobby, "as a little boy, you will have to act according to what you think men or little boys ought to be like. Self-definitions become your 'blankets.'"

"But don't you think of yourself as an old man?" asked Bobby, to whom anyone over the age of twenty seemed practically tottering on the edge of the grave.

"Not at all!" was Satyan's answer. "The age of this body is not *my* age. This body is much older than it seems, but in truth, I myself have no age. A person's true age takes him from time into timelessness."

"So then," Donny persisted, "the people in your time zone do things differently from one another not in order to *be* different, but just because, in themselves, they really *are* different—each one from all the others!"

"That's it!" said Satyan. "But now, I want you to listen to me carefully, for here comes a very important point: You've learned in your time travels that, while your effect on history is virtually non-existent, you *can* change yourselves by *observing* history. As you work on improving yourself, you discover increasingly that self-improvement means having a better attitude toward life: for example, being more kind to others, and more self-giving. Most people in your time zone don't realize that good attitudes like these are not just vague concepts: They depend also on the direction your energy flows in the body!"

"Do you mean that, when I give to others, my energy flows out to them?" Donny asked.

"Yes, partly I mean that, too. It helps to be aware *in oneself* of that outward, self-giving energy. But I mean something more, too. Tell me, for instance, Where do you feel love?"

"Well, gee," said Donny, "all over, I guess. In fact, when I think of how much I love Mother and Daddy, I'm not thinking of myself at all: I'm thinking of *them*."

"Of course," Satyan agreed. "But if at that time you turn your attention inward, to your own body, I think you'll notice, stirring there, a certain feeling. Where do you feel that stirring?"

"Well," Donny answered, "I've never given it a thought. I'm sure I don't feel anything stirring in my knees!"

"Do you feel anything in your heart?"

"Well, now that you mention it: yes! I do feel something there! Maybe especially when I'm enthusiastic or excited."

"That is where our emotions are centered," said Satyan. "Would you all like to join me in a little experiment?"

"Yes!" cried the three of them together.

"Then let's try this: Sit up straight." They did so. "Now, draw your shoulder blades together, forcing your concentration to that part of the body which lies between them: the heart." They did as he'd instructed. Bobby permitted himself a slight giggle. "Now then, chant a long-drawn-out 'A-ME-N!'" Bobby, reminded now of church, became more serious.

"Do you feel energy stirring in your hearts?" Satyan asked them.

"Yes, I do!" said Donny.

"So do I!" said Hansel.

"Good!" said Satyan approvingly. "Now then, try to direct that energy upward to the brain. As you do so, chant, 'Amen.'"

They performed the exercise. Satyan then added, "It might help you to think of that energy as a ray of moonlight reflecting upward from a little cup of water in your heart."

"Oh!" cried Bobby. "I *like* this!"

After a few more moments, Satyan interrupted their practice

to say, "Now, here's another thing I want to show you. When you think, 'I,' tell me, where is your energy centered."

"Is *that* in the heart, too?" Donny asked.

"It is indeed, in a deeper sense," Satyan replied. "But when you think of your *ego*, as distinct from other egos, where is your energy centered?"

They all looked at him blankly.

"Haven't you noticed how proud people hold their heads? Don't they tend to look down their noses at others? And haven't you noticed them draw their heads slightly backward?"

"Why, *yes!*" Donny marveled. "I've never really thought about it, but I *have* noticed that Mr. Maxwell, in Teleajen, holds his head that way. And *he's* certainly proud!"

"Is he ever!" exclaimed Bobby. "Only the other day he scolded me for not wiping my shoes before entering his house, and I wondered how he could even see me, his head was held up so high! I've noticed also that he seems to talk down at me, as if through his nose."

"That's because the seat of ego—that is, of your human self-awareness—is centered in what is called the medulla oblongata, at the base of the brain. When your energy is concentrated there, whatever ego-sense you possess will increase of its own accord. People who direct all their thoughts and actions from that point radiate their awareness outward from there. Thus, they separate themselves from everyone and everything else. It's like gazing out from a mountaintop onto a valley of mist. Nothing is clear, for everything becomes fogged over by self-consciousness. If, however, you could soar high above that peak, you'd see the world below you as a broad landscape: mountains, valleys, peaks, and broad plains: all one scene, and you yourself as a part of it all."

"How can we fly high into the sky?" asked Donny.

"There *is* a way!" Satyan replied. "The back of the head is the negative pole of self-awareness: our 'west.' The forehead is the 'east.'

"Now then, tell me," he continued, "when you feel inspiration, where is your energy centered?" Seeing puzzlement in Donny's eyes, Satyan continued: "For example, when you see a beautiful sunset, where in your own body are you most aware?"

"Well," said Donny, "but doesn't my energy go out to the sunset?"

"Yes, but *where in your body is it centered?*"

"I think that, in my body, my energy goes forward from the back of my head."

"Doesn't it flow upward as well as forward?"

"Well, yes, I suppose it does!" Donny exclaimed.

"Of course it does!" replied Satyan. "First it flows upward; and then forward. Between the eyebrows in your forehead lies the positive pole to the seat of ego in the medulla oblongata. If, from this negative pole, you focus your mind and *gaze at* that positive pole between the eyebrows, you will find in time that all your actions, reactions, thoughts, and observations radiate outward from *that* eastern center of your awareness."

"Wow!" Donny exclaimed. "It seems so simple!"

"It *is* simple! But it may take you years of practice for this effort not only to change you, but to uplift you into a new reality. When that happens—when your heart is uplifted, and when your seat of self-awareness shifts to the forehead—you'll be amazed to find that bliss suffuses your entire being!"

Donny: "Oh, *thank* you! What you've taught us seems to cap everything we've learned in our travels!"

"There's one more thing which the people in our time

zone are experimenting with. Convinced that there are many connections between the body and the mind, they are trying to discover whether certain bodily positions may not influence the mind and help one to develop certain beneficial attitudes."

"That certainly sounds interesting!" said Bobby.

"For example, when people feel positive or cheerful, don't they tend automatically to sit up straight? And when they're in a bad mood, don't they tend, rather, to slump forward?"

"Well, yes, I know it's true for me!" said Bobby.

"Well, sitting up straight may be a way of inducing your mind to develop more positive attitudes!"

Without thinking, his three guests sat up a little straighter and smiled.

"And now," said Satyan, "why do you tend to incline your head forward when you pray? I'll tell you: You are trying to relax the tension at the back of your head!"

"Wow!" Donny exclaimed.

"And why do you place your hands together when you pray? It's because you unconsciously want to offer your whole self up—from your very center."

"Gosh," said Donny, "I thought it was just a tradition."

"Well, the tradition is universal to all cultures. And how do such traditions begin? Most of them are founded on *some* reality that people unconsciously recognize.

"Some of our people," Satyan continued, "think that placing the palms together *behind* the back helps to develop devotion. That's something, however, I can't do anymore! This body won't let me. But why not try it?"

They did it, and all three said they felt a greater concentration of energy in the heart.

"When you join your palms high above the head," continued Satyan, "it helps to center you more inwardly.

"Well," he finished, withdrawing mentally into himself. "Enough of this! I only mentioned these things to add that some of our people are working at finding ways to position the body so as to help them raise their consciousness."

Donny now said, "Satyan, you promised me you'd show me how to fly up high."

"I thought you'd understand, Donny. I didn't mean you'd *literally* fly. I meant you'd learn to fly high *in consciousness*."

"Oh," replied Donny. "But it *would* be nice to be able to fly up into the sky."

"Why?" Satyan challenged him. "Birds do that, and are they better off than you, who can ask questions and grow in understanding? All birds do is flit about looking for worms!"

"You're right, Satyan. Whether I fly or don't fly, that's just another self-definition. I'm much better off learning to soar in consciousness."

"I'm very glad to see you working your way gradually out of your labyrinth of self-limitations," said Satyan.

They were standing in an open field. Just at that moment, a large disc appeared in the sky. It was what we today call a UFO, or, "Unidentified Flying Object." This one, however, didn't seem to be "unidentified" at all! Satyan exclaimed cheerfully, "Ah, I see that my friend Darshan has just returned."

The "flying saucer" landed gently on the grass before them. An opening appeared, and a ramp simultaneously descended from it to the ground. A man stepped out, and walked down the ramp.

"Satyan!" he cried, holding his arms wide with a glad smile. "It's been two years, I think?"

"Three," said Satyan. "I'm so happy to see you again! Where has your jaunt taken you this time?"

"To several planets in what we think of as the Pleiades!" replied his friend.

"And what did you see there?"

"Well, some of the planets seemed either to have rain all the time, or no rain at all! Not so pleasant! But I came upon one planet where the conditions were not only ideal, but the people, too, lived in a state of perfection that we have yet to attain here. There, they communicated easily with the inhabitants of the astral world. Their own bodies seemed to consist more of energy than of matter. And they welcomed me with great love. That's what took me so long: I didn't want to leave!

"There is so much I have to tell you about the life they lived. Children are born without sexual conception, and not from the bodies of their mothers. Baby forms appear, instead, by invitation from the astral world, materialized by a loving combination of masculine and feminine energy. In this way, parents get just what they want, and are in no likelihood of unintended surprises. What happens is that the mother welcomes into herself a loving inspiration from the father, sends out a call into the astral world for a soul karmically compatible with that inspiration, and, in cooperation with that soul, vibrates its consciousness more grossly into physical form.

"In the schools there, learning is not given intellectually, but is *absorbed*, spiritually, by the heart.

"Games are played by tossing balls of light high into the sky, then leaping onto them, riding them, and seeing (but not competitively) how many patterns they can form without falling off their light spheres.

"The people there live for hundreds of years. Illness is experienced only as a desire to leave one's body behind and merge in the consciousness of Infinity. While still on 'earth,' the inhabitants take delight in helping lower creatures to become more self-aware.

"I saw a little girl play with a worm. She whispered to it lovingly, 'Come on, little brother. I know you're self-aware. I know you *feel*. But try to become more *aware* of your feelings: try to feel *bliss!*'

"And then, believe it or not, the worm actually raised itself up a little and sort of shivered! I could almost *feel* its consciousness trying to smile!

"One day I met an old woman—at least, she said she was over two hundred years old, and their years are longer than ours. Yet her face wasn't deeply lined, and what lines there were showed that she'd lived her life in kindness, happily. There were no lines showing what people used to feel on our planet in former ages: lines of fatigue, bitterness, and disappointment. She was teaching a flock of birds to sing."

Bobby broke in at this point to ask: "Did the birds sing *melodies?*"

"Not melodies, as such," replied Darshan. "But they sang in rhythm, and seemed to understand what they were singing. I remember the song that she sang. It went:

Birds sing of freedom
    As they soar lightly on the air!
So may our hearts soar:
    High above all curbs and care!

"Next, they fluttered their wings, flew up from their branches, then circled enthusiastically about our heads. The woman smiled at me, remarking, 'You see? All creatures are expressions of the one bliss of God!'

"Well, as you can imagine, I was in no hurry to leave that place!"

"I can well imagine!" said Satyan. "But now your return will enrich all our lives, also."

For a long time, Hansel and the boys urged Darshan excitedly to tell them more about his travels to that world, and to other planets. It *seemed* a long time, but of course, in timelessness, no time passed at all.

"Satyan," Hansel said at last, "I think maybe it's time we stopped taking up more of your time in this timeless time zone!"

"So many times!" exclaimed Bobby with a smile. "But your timing this time, Hansel, does seem very timely."

"Thank you so very much, Sir," said Hansel, anxious for them not to seem too frivolous.

"You can thank me best by raising your own consciousness," replied Satyan. He added with a smile, "I am so happy you all came!"

Bobby was so enthusiastic about this visit that he embraced Satyan warmly. To his surprise, Satyan didn't respond, though he offered no resistance. Instead, he let his arms hang by his side.

"I never embrace people," he explained kindly. "It isn't because I don't love them. I simply feel more love for them if I don't clutch at them physically, as if trying to possess them."

Donny said, "Yet, when I hug Mother, it's because I love her."

"I understand. But there's also a higher love, which wants nothing for itself."

"I think I'd like to understand that love," said Donny thoughtfully. "Well, Satyan—Darshan," he concluded, "thank you from my heart!"

"Thank you both," said the others also. Hansel added, "It has given us a memory for a lifetime!"

They reentered their time-light spheres, scrolling them up, and, moments later, found themselves again on the grass outside the time tunnel.

"*That* was the best time trip of all!" exclaimed Donny.

"But the weirdest!" cried Bobby.

"I've never before visited that time zone," Hansel said. "I found it *very* enlightening."

"Tomorrow"—this from Donny—"will have to be our last adventure, Hansel. Mother is taking us back to Teleajen the day after."

"Oh, gee!" cried Bobby in disappointment. "I'd forgotten! What a wonderful summer this has been! I wish we could stay on forever."

"One hint of the reality of timelessness," said Hansel, "is that, whatever we find enjoyable, we wish it would go on forever and never end!"

"Well," Donny remarked, "let's try to have a very, *very* good time, tomorrow!"

"Yes, let's!" cried Bobby.

They bade goodbye to Hansel. Minutes later, they were swimming at their bathing hole in the brook. From there, they ran back to the inn.

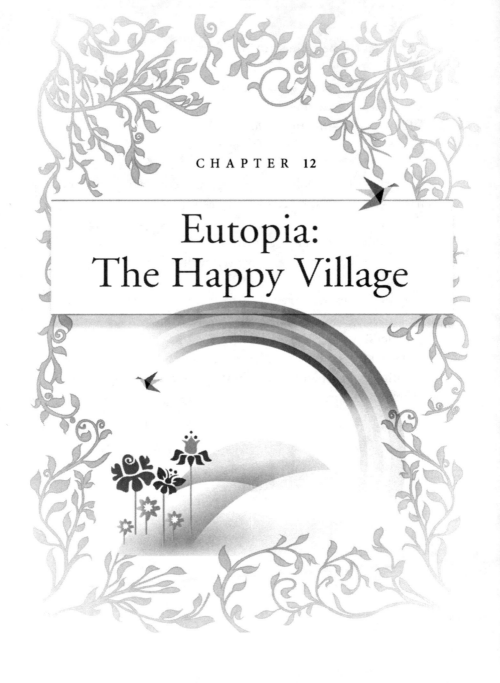

CHAPTER 12

Eutopia:
The Happy Village

"HAT'LL YOU DO, HANSEL," ASKED DONNY, "after we've gone back to Teleajen?"

"Here in the timeless NOW," Hansel answered, "I'm not really concerned. Nothing needs to happen at all for me to be completely contented."

"I know what you mean," responded Donny. "But back where we've come from, I know we've got only one more day. How shall we spend it? Where, in time, shall we travel?"

"Do you remember that brief glimpse we had of those mushroom-like villages?" Hansel asked. "Something calls me to visit there. Shall we give it a try?"

"Great!" cried Bobby. "They made me think of lots of little Teleajens!"

"They seemed so much nicer to live in than great cities like New York," was Hansel's comment. "But we'll have to go a little slowly, if we're to find the exact place in time."

Soon, they'd scrolled up their time-light spheres, and began to flow quickly through those bleak times when storm clouds and disasters covered the earth. Great cities crumbled and disappeared before their gaze. Huge tidal waves swept through the coastal cities. Volcanic eruptions swallowed up cities that were situated inland. Violent winds whipped across the earth, devastating the smaller towns. Earthquakes shuddered and shattered everything else. Small groups of people sat about,

143

here and there, in the shelter of trees, wearing only tattered rags for clothing and shivering in terror. Others huddled in muddy shelters which they'd dug into the ground.

Gradually, the sky cleared; the sun shone again. Green plant life began once again to cover the earth. It seemed as though, wherever our friends gazed, the earth was again coming to life. They proceeded for some time, passing through scenes of progressively greater beauty.

Their forward movement began to slow. Specific scenes began to chop across their vision. Suddenly, their time-light spheres stopped. The three travelers found themselves in a lovely garden behind a sweet-looking little home. Here they scrolled down their time-light spheres, and (again, as it were) stepped out into a springtime scene of graceful apple and cherry trees, covered with cheerful blossoms. A little brook ran through the garden, murmuring softly. Birds, most of them very small, sang happily everywhere.

A young woman came out of the house. I am aware that many authors describe their heroines in terms bordering on the fulsome. Other authors do, at least, show *some* restraint. But the rapturous ones, it seems to me, are always women. Why is that so? Do certain events in this story suggest a reason? The question takes on importance here because, as you'll see, this young woman is the only nubile maiden in my story. For starters, I will say only that she was pleasant to look at.

Oh, all right, to lower those raised eyebrows I'll add that she had green eyes, soft auburn hair, and a sweet smile. Enough?

She emerged from the back door of the house, and came over to them with that sweet smile.

"Welcome!" she said. She didn't whisper it. She didn't murmur it. She didn't coo, breathe, or sigh it. Nor did she even flute it.

She simply (forgive me) *said* it. But she *did* say it, and in a warm tone of voice.

"Welcome, strangers! Where did you pop in from?"

"We're as surprised as you are," said Hansel.

Hansel and she locked eyes. I think it's usually horns that get locked, but this was definitely a case of two people locking eyes. Both of them seemed to recognize something special in each other.

"We've come from very far away," Hansel said, "not in space, but in time."

She looked them over for a few moments appraisingly.

"Well," she concluded briskly, "you don't *look* like boneheads. So what's the game?"

"Let's just say we landed in your garden—I won't explain how."

After a brief pause, the girl shrugged. "Well, anyhow," she conceded, "you're here. What are your names?"

They told her, and then asked her hers.

"Jennifer," she replied.

To Donny, Bobby remarked in a whisper, "Not Gretel, you'll notice."

"And how may I make you welcome?" asked Jennifer.

"We'd certainly appreciate it," Donny piped up, "if you'd show us something of your village and your way of life here."

"Do you have any horses?" asked Bobby unexpectedly.

"There aren't any in this village," Jennifer replied. "But I have a dog. I'll introduce him to you later. First, though, let me take you around the outside of our home."

On the back side of the building, the entire wall depicted beautifully a large, brilliant rainbow arching over a countryside that contained flowery meadows, deep forests, and, high above the trees, mountains of which the upper slopes were covered in snow. The sides and front of the building were a deep crystalline blue, made from a substance which (curiously) conveyed a sensation of depth into which one could almost sink, while letting the imagination roam about freely in a mystical world. The roof was a gentle slope of turquoise blue, protruding out slightly from the building so as to make shade for the upper storeys.

The front of the house was partly hidden behind a veranda, the posts of which were constructed of that same crystalline blue. A screen around the porch lessened somewhat the over-all harmonious effect, but it obviously served the practical purpose of keeping out mosquitoes and other flying insects. The porch or veranda was garlanded, so to speak, by a profusion of roses.

As the guests glanced at other homes in the neighborhood, they noted that crystalline was the fashion here. The color of every house, however, was unique. The walls of one were a ruby red; of another, a luminescent yellow. All the basic colors of the rainbow were displayed profusely, and there were, in addition, many shades of in-between color, each one luminescent and beautiful.

"Before I take you inside and introduce you to my parents," said Jennifer, "there's something I'd like to get clear. Shall we sit here on the veranda for a moment?" She turned to Hansel. "I'd like to ask you. You seem of sound mind, and the thrill all three of you displayed while gazing at the homes in this neighborhood seemed quite genuine. But please tell me again now: *Where*—or *when*—did you say you'd come from?"

"From the early twentieth century," said Hansel, desperately anxious to win her good will, but at the same time wanting to answer her with complete truthfulness.

Jennifer closely scrutinized Bobby's eyes. "You're too young to tell a lie," she concluded. "Successfully, that is. Is Hansel telling me the truth?"

"That dead dinosaur in the forest looked awfully real!" insisted Bobby.

"Dinosaur! What on earth are you talking about?"

"Hansel built a time tunnel. We've been going backward and forward in time. He brought the dinosaur back from the Mesozoic Era. Fortunately, it died when he broke through the time barrier."

"Wait a minute! This is all too fantastic to be invented by *anyone*, let alone by a seven-year-old!"

"Seven and a half!" Bobby said indignantly, then quickly placing a hand over his mouth, he cried, "Oops! I forgot! That's a self-definition!"

"I give up! I'm completely bewildered," cried Jennifer.

"Hansel did build a time tunnel," Donny explained. "We've come through it into your time zone. We've been to other time zones, as well."

Jennifer looked at Hansel wonderingly, then, with growing respect, said, "You certainly *seem* sane!"

"I *want* you to believe in me," said Hansel. "But I just cannot tell you an untruth—and what you've just heard are the plain, absolute, unvarnished facts."

Jennifer stood up and invited our friends in through the front door. She waited there to observe their reactions as they entered.

"It looks so *different!*" cried Bobby the moment he came inside.

"Well, you should be used to *that*," said Donny.

"There are no lamps," Bobby exclaimed. "How," he asked, addressing Jennifer, "do you see to read at night?"

She looked closely at Bobby, then walked over to a wall and pressed what looked like a soft pad set into the wall. Suddenly that whole side of the room lit up, covering the whole wall with a soft light as if bathing it in sunlight.

"Wow!" cried Bobby.

"That surprises you?" asked Jennifer. "These lights are common everywhere in what you call our 'time zone.' Now then, won't you all please sit down?"

They went over and sat in three living room chairs. One of the chairs (the one Hansel selected) was straight-backed with no arms; the other two were armchairs, and looked more comfortable. Jennifer observed her three guests. The moment the boys seated themselves, they exclaimed loudly in astonishment.

"This amazement, surely, could not have been faked!" said the expression on Jennifer's face. The armchairs were too high for the boys' feet to touch the floor, and the seats extended too far forward for their knees to bend at the edges unless they sat forward, very upright, or stretched out halfway up their spines, with only their shoulders touching the seat backs. As soon as they sat down, however, the seats changed shape. The two boys found their feet resting on the floor, their knees bending at the edges of their seats, and their upper bodies resting snugly against the backs. In short order the armchairs had accommodated themselves to their young bodies.

Hansel's legs, on the other hand, were longer than most adults'. He found his seat rising to accommodate his greater height. He, too, seemed utterly astonished.

"Well," conceded Jennifer, "I don't see how you could have faked *that* astonishment! Especially Bobby."

Bobby inquired, "What *is* this time zone?"

"3053 AD," she told him.

"More than a thousand years after our time," Bobby commented. To Jennifer's surprise, he spoke quite casually.

"You should all have been shocked," was her comment. "*You* especially, Bobby, if your time zone was so long before our own.

Either you're pretending to have landed here now, or you really *haven't* lived here before."

"Well," said Bobby casually, "we *have* been moving about quite a lot!"

"Okay," said Jennifer. "Here's just one more test for you. I am something of a student of history. What year did you say you'd come from?"

"From the year 1935," said Bobby.

"So, then, Adolf Hitler was the dictator of Germany. You surely know that." The boys nodded; Hansel remained quiet, waiting to see what would come next. "What was the most important thing," continued Jennifer, "that happened under Hitler's dictatorship?"

"These boys haven't yet gone forward to that time zone, Jennifer," Hansel explained, "but I have. Hitler started a world war."

"Okay," said Jennifer, rather like checking on a student's responses in class. "But you might have assumed that fact from what already seemed probable in 1935. Now then, tell me, did he win or lose the war?"

"He lost it."

"Good enough. And what shocking event was it that finally ended the fighting?"

"Well, the war with Germany ended in the spring of 1945," said Hansel, "but the whole war was finally brought to a close in August of that year, when the United States of America dropped an atom bomb on Hiroshima."

"You're very convincing!" Jennifer concluded. "If you'd come from a later time zone, these boys, too, would have known about the war and that atom bomb. Coming from 1935, none of you could have known these things unless at least one of you had traveled forward in time." She sat back in her chair and exclaimed, "I'm absolutely astounded!"

"To us," said Donny, "the astounding thing is that we're even having this conversation. I mean, that we've actually told you where we come from."

"Normally," Hansel explained, "we try to seem contemporary with the people we meet in different time zones. In the last zone we visited, a man we met knew everything about us already. Otherwise, you're our first exception."

Jennifer sat staring at them in silence, scarcely able to absorb what she'd just heard. Meanwhile, the three of them gazed about, also in silence.

The shining wall remained lit. The boys whispered to each other that the chairs, apart from their amazing adaptability, were also beautiful. The fabric had no patterns. Somehow, the uniform colors were especially peaceful and soothing to the mind, and also to the heart's feelings. The colors were not bright, and seemed intended not to draw people's attention away from any conversation that was taking place in the room. The colors of the chairs were, for the most part, a muted but rich blue, reminiscent of the blue exterior walls of the house, but lighter in color. They blended well with the walls in the room, which were a delicate off-white rose. The ceiling was a purer white, brightly reflecting light from the wall into the room. The room contained no dining table, but a few steps on the far side of the room led up to what was, clearly, an area intended for dining. They saw there a table made not of wood, but of some rich indigo substance that was apparently meant (so Hansel whispered) to let the color of whatever food was eaten speak for itself. A light railing swept in an inward curve from the side of the upper area to a four-foot opening in the middle; the metal railing seemed put there to prevent anyone from losing his balance and falling into the room below.

The carpets bore woven designs, but these were limited mostly to the center of the carpet, with a few colors swirling also around the outer edges. The main color of some of the carpets was a rich, inviting red; others were a bright blue. The designs of all of them were a muted combination of orange, yellow, and lavender. The patterns displayed a pleasant symmetry, with lines shooting through them that were seemingly intended to draw people's gaze inward toward the center of the carpet. Altogether, each carpet evidently served the purpose of stimulating conversation without overwhelming it. Imbued into each weave was a sort of peaceful, reflective glow.

"Why aren't there any pictures on the walls?" asked Donny.

By now Jennifer was again ready to join the conversation. Smiling, she went over to a panel by the entrance to the room and pressed on a knob. Suddenly, three framed paintings appeared on the living room walls, and two more in the higher, dining area. The pictures, so the three visitors noted, were lit up from behind, as if emerging from the paintings themselves.

"We've a selection of many paintings," Jennifer explained. "Hundreds, I imagine, made by great, or at least excellent, artists, some of whom may be familiar to you; others were executed since your time. One thing you'll notice about them, however, is that they all deserve the description, '*friendly*.' My parents' first thought in selecting pictures has been to ask the question, 'Would we like to invite the artist, or the person he or she depicted, into our home?' Many classical paintings demonstrate artistic skill but give no hint of what are, to us, the most essential ingredients of all: upliftment, and inspiration. Few works, even of supposedly great art, are really inspired. Most of them demonstrate only excellent technique. By 'inspiration,'" Jennifer continued, "I mean feelings that uplift the heart."

"What a happy, happy home!" exclaimed Donny. "Happiness and beauty: these two qualities seem to define your whole village."

Bobby then reminded her, "You said you had a dog. Will we get to meet it?"

"It's a *him*," Jennifer corrected. "We wouldn't dare address Roquefort as an 'it'! I'll call him; he's upstairs. I'd also like to call my parents. They're in Daddy's study just now, working on a project. They're composing songs for children. Mummy's helping Daddy with the rhymes."

"*Roquefort!*" cried Bobby. "Why on earth did you name him *that*?"

"Well, we don't have Roquefort cheese nowadays, but I remember reading that it was a kind of spotty cheese, and our Roquefort has spots on the white part of his mane."

"Roquefort!" Bobby said in an undertone to Donny, giggling a little.

"Well," Donny commented with a smile, "at least it's memorable!"

Jennifer went upstairs and opened two doors. From the first there emerged a delighted collie, who came bounding downstairs, his long tail wagging exuberantly. The first person he went to friskily was Bobby, who patted him affectionately. Roquefort then approached Donny, got a friendly pat, and went over to Hansel, who stroked him a little distractedly.

Meanwhile, Jennifer had gone into another room on the ground floor. She returned with several sheets of paper and a bowl of blue powder. Placing a sheet of paper on the floor, she set the bowl of powder beside it. Roquefort went over to the paper, put a paw into the powder, and wrote on the paper in elaborate capital letters: "HOW YOU?" Then, wagging his tail, he looked at the three of them with what Bobby swore later on was an expectant smile.

"Oh, Roquefort!" cried Bobby appreciatively, "We're just fine! How are *you*?"

Roquefort, again with what certainly looked like a smile, wrote elaborately: "PLEASED."

He then bounded over to Bobby, and, using his teeth, pulled our little friend over to the bowl of powder. Dipping his paw once more into the bowl, he showed his affection for his new guest by placing a small dot of blue on Bobby's chest over the heart. He then licked the little boy's hand lovingly.

"Why, Roquefort," cried Donny, "won't you bless me, too?"

The dog came over and licked Donny's hand in a friendly manner. Evidently, however. his special blessing was meant above all for Bobby, to whom he quickly returned. He sat down and gazed at Bobby earnestly for some moments, focusing on the boy's eyes.

"I can't say how," Bobby explained later on to his brother, "but I *knew* Roquefort was sending me a message. It seemed to imply: 'You are as good as I. I am as good as you. All of us are equal to all others. And the goal of life is the same for everybody: to love one another, in God.'"

Moments later, Jennifer's parents appeared on the upper landing and descended the staircase. Both were smiling in welcome. The mother, whom Jennifer introduced as "My mother, Mrs. Ellington," gazed warmly at all three. Mr. Ellington grasped Hansel's hand warmly, then Donny's, then Bobby's. Donny looked at both the Ellingtons. To him, they appeared to be older versions of Jennifer.

"How do you account for that surprising similarity?" he asked Hansel in a whisper.

"Like attracts like," Hansel replied, also in an undertone. "Jennifer must have been born into this family because she already, in herself, shared with them many basic qualities."

"We're very happy to welcome you here!" said Mr. Ellington. "Where are you people from?"

Jennifer broke in hastily. "From the other side of nowhere, Daddy! They were strangers just passing through, and since they weren't from nearby I decided to make them feel at home."

"Quite right, Jenny," said Mr. Ellington. He didn't pursue the subject any further, but said only, "We're very happy to welcome all of you into our home."

"Daddy's been working on a project," Jennifer said. "Would you like to tell them about it, Daddy?" she smiled at him encouragingly.

"Indeed, yes!" her father replied. "We've only this morning completed a new song. Shall we sing it to you?"

"Oh, please *do*!" cried Donny.

"Well, here it is." The Ellingtons sang the song together.
Larks fly high in the summer sky,
> Regardless of the weather.
Even so we, too, can ascend up high
> As long as we soar together.
A kindly hand all can understand,
> And kindness helps awaken
Ev'ry thought of love that our souls demand
> When, for love, desires are mistaken.[2]

"Oh!" cried Donny, "that's *beautiful*! Can Bobby and I learn it? Will you teach it to us?"

---

* See the music notation for this song in the Appendix.

Mrs. Ellington sang it; then the four of them, including Jennifer, sang it with her.

"Daddy," said Jennifer, "are you sure about that last line? I'm not convinced all children will understand it."

"I know what you mean, Jenny," her father replied. "But I tried to improve on it, and couldn't. The song had to say something worthwhile, positive, and meaningful. I might have said something like, 'Ev'ry song of love that our dreams demand/ is a dream of love mistaken.' But that sentiment, sung by children, would fairly *reek* with disillusionment. The teachers can, and of course will, explain the lyrics to them. The children will then understand from the song that true love is self-giving, and isn't linked to selfish desires. Moreover, the melody itself is upbeat: it isn't at all sad or cynical."

"In fact, Daddy, it's an essay in itself. And it's also fun to sing! I do think children will love it." Jenny then whispered to Hansel as an aside: "You do see that I'm needed here, don't you? I'm useful to them as an anchor!" She smiled.

"Our schools are a very important part of our way of life here," Mrs. Ellington said. "Long ago our people abandoned the sterile concept that the main purpose of schooling is to train children to get good jobs when they grow up, and to earn good money."

"Everyone on earth really wants only one thing," said Hansel: "happiness. In that search, money can be a blind alley—promising much, but faithful in only one way: It *always* breaks its promises!"

Jennifer looked at him wide-eyed. "That's *marvelous!*" she exclaimed enthusiastically.

"It's the simple truth," affirmed Hansel.

"We try to inculcate that thought into our children," she said, "but it isn't always easy. We offer precepts, and Daddy writes songs that contain practical teachings, but somehow theory can't stand up to experience. If the children get emotionally upset, or if they see something they want and decide that's *all* they want, it's difficult to rein in their feelings. Telling them to behave just doesn't do it for them. By the time they've grown up, most of them do in fact manage pretty well, but it's not an easy job, bringing them to that point."

"Have you tried letting them teach themselves?" Hansel inquired.

"What do you mean? They can only learn from people who know more than they do."

"Yet I've found in my travels that most people are wiser than they think."

"Why don't we go together to our local school?" Jennifer proposed. "I'd like you to see how it functions."

Hansel assented. They left the house together. Donny and Bobby, for the first time, remained behind. They'd found a picture book depicting other villages in this time zone.

As Hansel and Jennifer walked down the street, a number of villagers smiled at them warmly. Some of them walked in little groups; a few went in pairs; one or two walked by themselves. From time to time Jennifer stopped to greet someone, and introduced Hansel also. The conversations were all friendly and mutually exhilarating.

"Has this village a name?" Hansel asked.

"We call it Eutopia," replied Jennifer. "'Utopia' would mean 'no place,' but 'Eutopia' means a place of beauty and harmony."

"How perfect!" was Hansel's comment.

Upon reaching the school, they entered the grounds. Within moments they came upon a class being held under a tree out of doors. The teacher looked at them, smiled, then continued her lesson.

"When Sir Philip Sidney received a severe wound on the battlefield," she said, "someone brought him a desperately needed drink of water. A soldier of low rank lay nearby, close to dying. Sidney told his assistants to give that soldier the water they'd brought for him. As he put it, 'This man's need is greater than mine.'

"What do you get from this story, children?" the teacher asked.

One child raised his hand. "The story teaches me," he hazarded, "that it is noble to sacrifice for others."

"Very good!" said the teacher.

"Pardon me," whispered Hansel to Jennifer. "Would it be all right if I interrupted?"

"After what you've been telling me," replied Jennifer, "I think we'd all welcome anything you have to say."

"Well then," he raised his voice, addressing the teacher, "may I say something?"

"By all means," she replied, seeing him there beside Jennifer, who, it seemed, was held in high regard by everyone.

"Why don't we try learning that same lesson from real life?" asked Hansel. "May I try to do so?"

Receiving the teacher's consent, Hansel singled out a little girl in the class, and asked her to stand up. "What is your name?" he asked.

"My name is Rachel," the child said with a timid smile.

"Now then, Rachel, tell me first: *Why* is it noble to sacrifice for others?"

"Gee," said the little girl, "I guess being noble makes everyone look up to you."

"There's another, even better reason," Hansel suggested. "Sacrifice is noble because it makes *you*, yourself, feel good inside! Why don't we talk about *you*—you, right here, today?

We haven't an actual situation here, because situations like this happen unpredictably. But let's pretend your mother has wrapped a very special treat today for your lunch. Can you think of anything extra special that you'd like?"

Smiling, Rachel said—yes, believe it or not, she actually did say, "Apfelstrudel"! Hansel continued with a smile (he had, after all, his own fond memories of that particular delicacy!), "All right: You're looking forward to enjoying it, aren't you?"

"Yes, of course I am!" Rachel answered.

"However," Hansel then said, "just before lunch you see a boy crying his heart out. I don't know what he's crying about; maybe someone tripped him and he fell; or maybe somebody said something that hurt his feelings. Anyway, you *know* he'd feel much better if you gave him a piece of that Apfelstrudel. What would you do?"

"Oh, my!" said Rachel, "I'm not sure I'd want to share it with him. Certainly I wouldn't want to give him very much of it!"

"Now then," pursued Hansel, "imagine enjoying it all by yourself. Once it's finished it's finished, isn't it? You can't enjoy it any more. But now imagine something else: if you share some of your Apfelstrudel with that boy, his gratitude to you will last a long time, won't it? Maybe you'll find you've even made a friend of him for life. Think carefully about the choice before you. Visualize the scene. Then visualize its alternatives. See everything very clearly in your mind. Can you see anything attractive about giving him a piece of that strudel?"

"Oh, yes, I see it clearly!" cried Rachel. "Having a sincere friend would mean *much* more to me!"

"Right, I think so too," commented Hansel. "Now then, think of the pleasure you'd get from sharing at least a part of that Apfelstrudel with him; then ask yourself: 'Could I give it *all* to him?' Think of his need, and of how much it would mean to him, in his grief, to receive such a gift from you. Then think how fleeting your own enjoyment of that sweet would be, if you ate all or most of it yourself. If you gave it to him, it would not only be a gift of the dessert: It would be a gift of lasting happiness. Wouldn't *that* mean something to you?"

"Oh, now that you put it that way," said Rachel, "I can see the point clearly: My own happiness would be *much* greater if I treated him kindly!"

"And so, don't you think that the reward of increased happiness for your great act of kindness would make the act of giving very much worthwhile to you?"

"Oh, *yes!*" exclaimed Rachel.

Hansel turned to the teacher. "You see?" he said. "Giving children a selfish motive for being unselfish is the best way to wean them from their natural egoism. They can't be told to be *un*selfish. The only good we can ever know is what we consider good *for ourselves*."

Doubtfully the teacher answered, "But that seems hypocritical! If I only *pretend* I'm doing good to others, though really seeking my own good, where's the virtue in it?"

"There is enlightened selfishness," Hansel explained, "and there's unenlightened selfishness. Other peoples' pleasure, for each of us, is vicarious. The only honest attitude we can have is to realize that kindness to others makes *us*, ourselves, happier. That is why Jesus said, 'It is more blessed to give than to receive.' It's 'more blessed,' because it makes one more blissful!"

Later, as Hansel and Jennifer were leaving the school grounds, she exclaimed, "You're a marvel! I think in those few minutes you taught the children, and the teacher too, more about the art of happy living than they could have learned in a year."

"And yet," Hansel said, "this *is* a happy village. The people I've seen here seem to share willingly with one another. Looking about me, I am very well impressed."

"Yes, we are open to these thoughts, but it helps to have them spelled out for us so clearly. Shall we get back now to the others? I'd like to share with Daddy and Mummy what you've just taught me."

"I mentioned Jesus Christ in my little talk," said Hansel. "I am sure Christianity continues to thrive in this time zone. But do you still have denominations? Catholics, Protestants, and the rest of them?"

"From my studies of history," Jennifer replied, "I know what you mean. But, no, we have no denominations, as such, here. Nor do we have competing religions. Our faith isn't based on mere beliefs. We know that divine truth is far more universal than the facts science tried for so long to wrest from Nature. Today, we *know* that Love is higher than reason, and bestows deeper insight into reality. We know that God is everywhere, and that He *is* everything. We know that He isn't a '*He.*' 'He,' as people once called him, is our Father, Mother, Friend, Beloved— our Everything! The entire universe is a manifestation of 'His' consciousness."

They returned to Jennifer's home, and found Bobby there, romping in the garden with Roquefort. Donny was indoors, talking seriously with her mother.

"We were discussing this village," Donny said, when they entered the house. "It seems such a perfect place to live in. The big cities that once infested the earth gave rise to so many emotional diseases: pride, competitiveness, indifference to others' feelings. Narrow selfishness festered in them, and a spirit of fierce greed. People tried to snatch from one another every teaspoon of happiness they could seize for themselves."

Mrs. Ellington welcomed her daughter and Hansel with a

smile. "What a bright little boy Donny is!" she cried. "He's been saying that the most important thing in life is to improve ourselves."

"We can also learn from others *how* to change ourselves," said Jennifer. "Mummy," she continued, "Hansel would be *such* a great help in our school! I'm planning next year, as you know, to become a teacher, though I've never liked the term, 'schoolteacher.' I'd rather be called a 'children's teacher': it sounds more friendly and personal, since after all it isn't the *school* I'll be teaching, but the children! But wouldn't it be wonderful if Hansel and I could teach together? We share the same ideals."

"Dear Boy," her mother replied kindly, addressing Hansel. "The moment I first laid eyes on you, you seemed to me the son I never had."

"Oh, *Mummy*! That is what I feel, too," cried Jennifer. "It's as though he were our own!"

Hansel took Jennifer's hand and pressed it warmly. "Is there a chance," he said, "that we might spend our lives together? When I'm with you, I feel so much *happiness*! *Would* you marry me?"

"Dear *Son*!" cried Mrs. Ellington, who already saw him in that light.

"Daddy!" Jennifer called out. Her father emerged from an upstairs room and leaned down over the bannister.

"What is it, Jenny?"

"Daddy, would you please come down here?"

Mr. Ellington came and joined them.

"Daddy, Hansel wants me to marry him!"

Her father's kindly face puckered in a slight frown. "Do you really think you can make such an important decision without careful forethought?"

"Oh, Daddy, when you know, you *know*!"

"Well, child," he answered, "I felt good about him the moment I first met him. There's merit, certainly, in catching a train while it's still in the station!"

"Oh, *Daddy!*" cried Jennifer in mock-stern disapproval. "Hansel isn't a *train!*"

"Well, dear, let me have my little joke! But yes, you have my wholehearted blessing. Besides, it has often occurred to me that it might be better for the man to come to the woman, rather than the reverse. Many societies have insisted on the woman going to the man, but what I've often thought is this (and I'm not being personal): When the woman goes to the man, she may have to plod like a workhorse under the whip of a jealous mother-in-law, who feels she has prior claims on her son. But when the man comes to the woman, his mother-in-law is more likely to adopt him lovingly as her son.

"Again, when the woman comes to the man, she is brought into *his* home, to his sometimes-resentful relatives, as well as to a father who may have plans of his own for his son's future, which he may see as a means of fulfilling his own desires. It happens all too often that sons who live under the influence of their fathers never get to fulfill their own dreams. When a young man lives under the influence of his wife's family, however, her father is more likely to accept him as a partner, and not to make emotional demands of him."

Hansel added, "Well, I really haven't much to go back to, anyway. For me, this is the best possible solution."

He and Jennifer embraced lovingly, then looked about them with radiant, happy smiles. At that moment Bobby entered the room accompanied by Roquefort, who went and stood before Jennifer. Looking up at her, he gave a brief bark, whereupon she went and fetched him another piece of paper, laid it on the carpet, and placed the bowl of blue powder beside it.

In large letters, Roquefort wrote out laboriously with his right paw: "PLEASED!"

Bobby, standing nearby, said, "Am I sniffing something in the air?"

"Molasses!" whispered Donny. "Sweet, but sticky!" Aloud he said, "It looks like we'll be going back to Teleajen leaving no thread untied. But Hansel, how do you expect to shift to this new time zone? You know that isn't possible."

"Yet we've already seen two occasions," Hansel protested, "when we were able to affect people's lives by love, even if they lived in time zones far removed from our own. My love for Jennifer has given me a new revelation: It *is* possible, by the same power of love, to change one's time zone!"

"Teleajen ho! then," said Bobby with a broad grin.

"Forgive us," Donny said, addressing Jennifer and her parents. "We came, as you told your father, 'out of nowhere.' It's time for us to return to that 'nowhere.'"

Roquefort went to Hansel and nudged his stomach, as if with approval. Hansel fondly embraced him, then hugged both the boys. "We've had some *wonderful* adventures together!" he exclaimed.

"Wonderful—and *so instructive!*" cried Donny. "We'll always remember you in our hearts, Hansel." Tears shone in his eyes. "I hope we'll be welcome, if we ever visit here again?"

"Oh, much *more* than welcome!" Hansel cried. "Please come again. Come *often!*"

The boys left the house by the front door, walked to a spot beyond the village, and reached an almost empty field, though in full view of a small herd of cows, and there paused in preparation for re-creating their time-light spheres. The cows gazed at them incuriously, as if asking themselves whether the intruders wanted to access their grass.

The boys were soon back at the sward outside the time tunnel, then at Frau Weidi's in Timiș, and then in the car, the next day, accompanying their mother back to Teleajen.

Did they ever—you ask?—return to Timiș, and to the ruined laboratory? Did they ever again enter the time tunnel? Did they travel forward again to 3053 AD, to Eutopia (that ideal "somewhere"), and to Hansel, Jennifer, Roquefort, and the Ellingtons? I wish I could say, "Of course they did!" Destiny, alas, doesn't always give us what we want in life. It took Donny and Bobby far afield.

In 1935, World War II was already looming on the horizon. The two boys were sent away to school in England, far from Romania. In 1939 they sailed with their parents by ship to America, for what they imagined would be only a vacation. That year, however, Germany invaded Poland, and started the Second World War. The two boys grew older, and became men. Alas, they never returned to Romania, or to Transylvania. Bobby raised a charming family of his own; Donny, no longer young now, never had a family. I suspect he won't ever return to the legendary scene of his childhood.

But a question remains: Will *you* go there?

THE END

Appendix

Larks Fly High

Donald Walters

light and playful

1. Larks fly high in the sum - mer sky, Re - gard - less of the weath - er. E - ven so we, too, can as - cend up high, As long as we soar to - geth - er.

2. A kind - ly hand all can un - der - stand, And kind - ness helps to wak - en Ev - 'ry thought of love that our souls de - mand When, for love, de - sires are mis - tak - en.

About the Author

Swami Kriyananda

Swami Kriyananda founded and leads the world's largest network of intentional communities and has overseen the establishment of five schools, the well-known East West Bookshop chain, three publishing houses, three world-renowned retreat centers, and a number of other small businesses, all of which continue to thrive and grow. He has composed over 400 pieces of music and written more than 100 books, which have sold over 4 million copies and are translated into 29 languages.

CRYSTAL CLARITY PUBLISHERS

Crystal Clarity Publishers offers many additional resources that combine creative thinking, universal principles, and a timeless message.

For our online catalog, complete with secure ordering, please visit us on the web at:

www.crystalclarity.com

To request a catalog, place an order for the products you read about in the Further Explorations section of this book, or to find out more information about us and our products, please contact us:

Crystal Clarity Publishers
14618 Tyler Foote Rd., Nevada City, CA 95959
TOLL FREE: 800.424.1055 or 530.478.7600 / FAX: 530.478.7610
EMAIL: clarity@crystalclarity.com